GIRL IN THE LAKE

A DETECTIVE CHARLOTTE PIERCE MYSTERY

NAMELESS GIRL
BOOK 3

KATE GABLE

COPYRIGHT

Visit my website at www.kategable.com

BE THE FIRST TO KNOW ABOUT MY UPCOMING SALES, NEW RELEASES AND EXCLUSIVE GIVEAWAYS!

Want a Free book? Sign up for my Newsletter!

Sign up for my newsletter:

https://www.subscribepage.com/kategableviplist

Join my Facebook Group:
https://www.facebook.com/groups/833851020557518

Bonus Points: Follow me on BookBub and
Goodreads!

https://www.goodreads.com/author/show/21534224.
Kate_Gable

ABOUT KATE GABLE

Kate Gable loves a good mystery that is full of suspense. She grew up devouring psychological thrillers and crime novels as well as movies, tv shows and true crime.

Her favorite stories are the ones that are centered on families with lots of secrets and lies as well as many twists and turns. Her novels have elements of psychological suspense, thriller, mystery and romance.

Kate Gable lives near Palm Springs, CA with her husband, son, a dog and a cat. She has spent more than twenty years in Southern California and finds inspiration from its cities, canyons, deserts, and small mountain towns.

She graduated from University of Southern California with a Bachelor's degree in Mathematics. After pursuing graduate studies in mathematics, she switched gears and got her MA in Creative Writing and English from Western New Mexico University and her PhD in Education from Old Dominion University.

Writing has always been her passion and obsession. Kate is also a USA Today Bestselling author of romantic suspense under another pen name.

Write her here:

Kate@kategable.com

Check out her books here:

www.kategable.com

Sign up for my newsletter:
https://www.subscribepage.com/kategableviplist

Join my Facebook Group:
https://www.facebook.com/groups/833851020557518

Bonus Points: Follow me on BookBub and Goodreads!

https://www.bookbub.com/authors/kate-gable

https://www.goodreads.com/author/show/21534224.Kate_Gable

ALSO BY KATE GABLE

All books are available at ALL major retailers! If you can't find it, please email me at
kate@kategable.com
www.kategable.com

Detective Kaitlyn Carr

Girl Missing (Book 1)
Girl Lost (Book 2)
Girl Found (Book 3)
Girl Taken (Book 4)
Girl Forgotten (Book 5)

Girl Hidden (FREE Novella)
Lake of Lies (FREE Novella)

Detective Charlotte Pierce

Last Breath
Nameless Girl
Missing Lives
Girl in the Lake

Lake of Lies (FREE Novella)

ABOUT GIRL IN THE LAKE

Hidden secrets and deadly lies...

Following the incident that nearly killed her boyfriend, **Detective Charlotte Pierce needs a weekend away** with him in the quaint **mountain town of Quail Lake, California.**

However, their trip is interrupted **when a sixteen-year-old camp counselor goes missing. The girl's body** is later found by the lake shore **with strangulation marks** around her neck and bruises all over.

The sleepy town of Quail Lake has only one inexperienced deputy on call and Charlotte can't say no when the sheriff asks her to help with the investigation.

When she begins to speak to the girl's roommates and crush as well as other camp counselors, Charlotte's instincts tell her that this wasn't a drifter who had committed this **terrible murder**. This was someone who was close to her. **But who would want such a nice girl dead?**

As Charlotte continues to investigate, she discovers that Camp Quail Lake is full of **secrets and lies. Nothing is what it seems and everyone has a reason to keep their stories to themselves.**

From the exciting beginning to its various **twists and turns,** the novel will keep you guessing all the way to the end. **Girl in the Lake** is a stark reminder that **summers don't last forever, secrets can't stay buried and but murderers kill for a reason.**

Praise for Kate Gable's Girl Missing Series

"Gripping! This book was a great read. I found a new author that I enjoy and I can't wait to read the rest of the series! " *(Goodreads)*

"The twists come at you at breakneck pace. Very suspenseful." *(Goodreads)*

"I really enjoyed the ins and outs of the storyline, it kept me reading so that I could find out how the story would turn out. And the ending was a major shocker, I never saw it coming. I truly recommend this book to everyone who loves mysteries and detective stories." *(Goodreads)*

⭐⭐⭐⭐⭐" I loved it. One of the best books I've ever read." - Amazon review

⭐⭐⭐⭐⭐ "I couldn't put the book down I give it a thumbs up and I would recommend it to other readers" *(Goodreads)*

⭐⭐⭐⭐⭐ "Another great book in the Kaitlyn Carr series! I am so drawn into these books. I love that they are not just about Kaitlyn's search for her sister but also about a case she is working on. I can't wait for the final book in the series!" *(Goodreads)*

PROLOGUE

I meant to get out early, but I slept in, dragging myself out of bed with Dylan still snoring. I put on a T-shirt and shorts, laced up my sneakers, and stepped outside. It's mid-morning now, around nine o'clock, but the birds are still chirping, the insects are still buzzing, and the clear blue water is calling my name.

Still, my body resists the call. I drag my legs out of the cabin. I had just woken up, but I know that the exercise will do me some good. I've gotten into the groove of running a little bit at a time. When I'm not running, I'm walking, just getting the steps in. It feels good to be alone first thing in the morning, engaging my body. Instead of placing pressure on myself to run a certain amount I just walk or run, listen to whatever I want to on YouTube, a podcast, an audiobook, anything at all.

I love the freshness of the air up here. It's at least twenty degrees hotter down in the desert but just being in the relative cool for a couple of days is enough to reset, recalibrate. This is exactly what I wanted.

I don't even mind; in fact, I enjoy that Dylan is not here. It's a little bit of time alone with my thoughts and my body. Looking out onto the shore of the lake there is nothing but blue water, pine trees, and a rocky shoreline just behind me. I get a stitch in my side at my waist and bend over in half to gather my breath. My AirPods stop cooperating or maybe the internet connection isn't great, so I pull them out of my ears. I suddenly hear a voice out in the distance.

"Help! Help!" a woman yells, waving her arms at me.

Despite the stitch, I push myself forward into a loping run, not sprinting, but faster than I would have run for exercise.

Quail Lake is surrounded by a glacier meadow with smooth, silky grasses embedded into the forest floor, broadening widely all around. I run along the mossy bogginess of the rocky shore, rough in parts, weedy in others. These meadows are where the butterflies and flowers make their home as close to the beginning of the water as possible.

The beach runs for some distance, cleared out a bit for swimming where the moss rarely gathers on the smooth stones and boulders. Here, the sod is plushy and crowded with daisies, gentians, and various species of grass, as well as an explosion of flowers and butterflies. It's hard to describe the exquisite beauty of this carpet that lines the lake, none of which I notice as my heart speeds up and I race toward the woman in need of help. Her waving slows down a little bit as I get closer. Then she seems to let out a sigh as I approach her.

"I found a girl. She's dead!" the woman yells and points to the legs of a young woman. Her head is being caressed lightly by the wavelets at the edge of the lake. I rush up to her and take her pulse, immediately hating to confirm the fact that she is, indeed, gone.

1

SARAH

On a bright sunny morning, nobody would know that this day would be different from any other except for Sarah Dunn.

She woke up with darkness in the pit of her stomach. She checked the box next to her bed to make sure that all her earthly possessions were in one place.

They were.

Then she wrote in her journal, just like she did every morning to organize her thoughts and to record what she's thinking about.

Tomorrow, she would be seventeen years old, and her last day as a sixteen-year-old would mean a lot.

How would she spend it?

She was a camp counselor so much of the day was planned out for her, which she liked.

Summer birthdays were hard because your friends weren't at school. They were busy with their own lives.

A camp at Quail Lake provided the structure that she never knew that she craved, a routine that she lacked at home.

Her mom was on her second husband. Her dad had a new girlfriend every week.

The one thing they agreed upon was that they would pay for her private school and that they would send her to camp all summer. They probably just wanted to get her out of the house, but Sarah didn't care. She might have resented it when she was younger, but now that she was a counselor, she had a job that she was proud of.

Sarah was an early riser who always woke up way before her roommates.

On this particular day, she had nothing of importance to write in her journal and just noted the weather and the fact that she woke up with a heavy heart, but hoped that it would change throughout the day.

The one thing she was worried about was getting older.

Even though she was only sixteen, she was dreading turning eighteen, nineteen, twenty, twenty-five.

She was dreading becoming an adult because it was already so hard being a kid. She wasn't sure she could handle the additional stresses.

Her parents didn't expect much from her.

College, a nice wedding to invite their friends to, the big family.

Mom had already started talking about it even though Sarah had never even had a boyfriend. Actually, the fact that she'd never had a boyfriend seemed to be the only thing that worried her mom at all.

She had put Sarah on birth control pills when she was thirteen so that she would be safe.

Little did she know that her daughter had never even been kissed.

Sarah had a crush on a boy at camp, Dominic Marcel, a counselor for the boys' section who was an excellent swimmer and worked mainly as a lifeguard at the lake.

She once joked that, "The only reason you took that job was to ogle all the girls," and when she said that he gave her a wink and a nod, and she knew she was right.

All the girls at camp loved him because he had that sexy smile, that nice tan, and that 'I-don't-give-a-crap' attitude that is so attractive about teenage boys.

TODAY WAS the last day that she would be sixteen years old. If she were to make a wish, her wish would be to get kissed before she turned seventeen. She had been around her bunkmates long enough to know that they had all done that, and a lot more, with their casual guy friends and occasional boyfriends, and suspected that one of the main reasons they came to camp was to hook up with the counselors from the boys' section.

She hated to admit it, but just like everyone else, Dominic was the one that she liked the most. He wasn't arrogant or full of himself like his friend, Aaron. He was very easy on the eyes and had a casual demeanor that made everyone want to be his friend.

In the bathroom, she looked at herself in the mirror. Dark auburn hair down her back, hazel eyes, freckles, the ones she always hated as a kid but had since developed a mild appreciation for. There were even TikTok videos about how to apply makeup to the bridge of your nose to make it look like you have freckles. Finally, her look was being appreciated, but not soon enough to take all that self-hatred out of her mind.

Sarah put some eyeliner around the top of her eyes, filled in her eyebrows a little bit like she had just learned to do a couple of weeks ago, and applied a good dose of sunscreen, because unlike her bunkmates, she always burned way too easily and never tanned. She pulled her hair up into a loose, high-fitting ponytail and straightened out her shoulders, trying to remind herself to stand up straight and not slouch so much. As soon as she walked away from the mirror, she'd found herself hunched over a little bit, her natural pose.

The glasses that she wore on her nose didn't make life any easier at camp. They weren't the kind that you wore just for social media to make yourself look smart. These were necessary. Despite how much her mom asked her if she wanted to get contacts, she couldn't bear putting her finger in her eye, and couldn't even consider LASIK surgery. So she was stuck with these thick oval-shaped ones that always created separation between her and the world.

The cool way to wear them would be somewhere near the tip of her nose, but that would make it almost impossible for her to see anything far away, which is why she wore them in the first place. She wore them close to her eyes. Her mascara, not entirely dried yet, left marks on the glass that she would have to later wipe off.

Breakfast would not be for a while, at six thirty, so she decided to go for a walk. She crept out of the cabin and headed outside, holding the door so that it didn't slam or squeak, waking up her friends.

The other three girls in the cabin continued to sleep peacefully, faces turned away from the front door, buried under pillows and blankets. She knew that if they hadn't been to camp together for years, they would probably not be friends.

Elizabeth was tall and popular, with long legs and a print modeling contract. Bennett was smart and strong, ranked second in the country for crew and had almost a guaranteed spot on the Harvard crew team, just like her mom. Elizabeth and Sarah, both went to private schools, but different ones, in Southern California, while Bennett attended a big blue ribbon, highly ranked public school with tons of celebrity kids. Then there was Tony, the one girl who was most likely to be her friend outside of camp. She was similarly bookish, but not particularly good at test taking. Ordinarily she would be destined to go to a second-tier college, except for the fact that her parents were both USC alums and, despite the noise that schools like that made about moving away from legacy admissions, she would probably be a shoo-in there.

She wore all black, was from Northern California, and they kept in touch the most when they were apart. What Sarah didn't know was how socially minded Tony would become during this past year. She talked about it enough when they FaceTimed but kept the specifics to herself.

Sarah would never admit this out loud, but Tony made her feel better about herself. She was overweight, with short frizzy hair that she could never get under control. Next to her, Sarah looked gorgeous, and she liked being in pictures with her instead of Elizabeth and Bennett, who towered over her. Her hair was always perfect. The clothes were always on trend.

It wasn't that Sarah didn't care about the causes that Tony did. It was just that she didn't want to spend the summer or her school days creating petitions and organizing people for causes that hadn't been changed in the last forty years, while Bennett and Elizabeth apparently couldn't care less about any of that stuff and found Tony's interest mildly amusing.

KATE GABLE

Sarah felt like she had to pay attention. She had to engage, but she didn't really want to.

As Sarah slipped out of the cabin that morning, the birds chirped above her head, and the sun had just come up. Sunrises were glorious on the lake, but few people took advantage of them, given the long hot day ahead.

Out in the distance, she saw him, sitting on the edge of the dock, his feet submerged in water, his head bopping up and down to the faint music coming from his phone.

2

CHARLOTTE

Summers have a distinctive smell because of the heat that comes off the sidewalk. When you walk under an overarching oak tree, the small breeze picks up your hair and tosses it in your face. Bees buzz around all the blooming flowers and the neighborhood is filled with the smells of citrus, life, and hope.

The new year begins when summer comes. At least that's what I always used to believe. It's like a rejuvenation in nature, and I don't even live anywhere where it's particularly cold. In the deserts, the summers are long and hot. People tend to escape to the ocean or up to the mountains.

Dylan and I are driving up the winding, curvy road to Quail Lake, about an hour and a half drive from home. The last time I was here, about six weeks ago, I was working a case, but today, we're on vacation. Five glorious days off and nothing but bright blue skies, a crystal-clear lake, and seventy-five degree weather to enjoy.

The pines are starting to get taller and taller and when we stop at an overlook, the orange desert, punctuated by rows and rows of palm trees, spreads out in all directions below us. It's the place I call home but also the place that I won't miss for a weekend.

Dylan's recovery is going a lot faster and smoother than anyone thought. After he was transferred home, I helped take care of him. His parents came as well and helped us with whatever he needed: dinners, groceries, and everything else since I was still working my crazy hours. Due to his injuries, Dylan is off for a couple of months at least.

He moved into my house, because it was bigger, so that everyone had a room. His parents left a couple of weeks ago, and it was just the two of us, and he no longer needed so much daily care. He could walk around on his own. To give him credit, he's been really pushing the boundaries of his recovery; walking as much as he can every day, even trying to lift weights, basically making recovery his full-time job.

"I'm really looking forward to this trip," Dylan says as we pull up to a small one-bedroom cabin overlooking the lake. "Wow, this is amazing. Look at this view. Thank you so much for getting it."

"Well, let's hope that it's not completely a shambles inside," I say. "Sometimes the listings can really exaggerate how nice they are."

"Don't be silly," he says, giving me a squeeze. "It's going to be great. Whatever it is."

We park in the small driveway and walk up the stairs. He insists on carrying both of our heavy backpacks filled with laptops, chargers, and all the other electronics we can't be without.

The expansive patio that wraps three-quarters of the way around has a beautiful view of the lake in all its bright blue glory.

"I can't wait to go down there," I say.

We paid extra to not have to cross the road that circles the lake. All it requires is a walk down the narrow trail and we are at the sandy beach below. We stay on the porch, taking in the view, watching an eagle fly by as well as a couple of large mountain ravens. I hear the honking of some geese down by the water and I know that I found the perfect place for our little getaway.

"I'm so glad that you were able to take this time off," Dylan says. "It's well deserved."

"I was getting a little overwhelmed with the cases and the workload. I thought that's why I left LAPD, right?"

"Well, you don't control these things, especially when everyone else is out, but you really deserve to relax. These five days are going to be glorious."

"Yes." I nod. "Amazing."

We walk inside and we're greeted by tall ceilings, an open concept cabin, floors, walls, and ceilings made of knotty pine, and a reclining couch facing the TV and the view of the lake.

"Look at that. You can sit here watching Netflix and still get a nice view."

"I know. I can't wait," Dylan says, wincing a little bit as he puts down the backpacks.

We haven't been intimate since his accident, and that's another thing that both of us are undoubtedly looking forward to. Spending some romantic time together.

The bedroom is to the side of the living room but has a similarly expansive view of the lake since it has French doors that open onto the porch and a bay window on the far side. The tall ceilings with the fan make it the perfect temperature.

I tell Dylan to wait here, not to bother going up and down the stairs while I get the rest of our stuff. He tries to protest, but I tell him that I don't need him getting hurt and he can help by making lunch. As bad as the pain has been, Dylan has struggled more with not being useful. It takes a couple of trips up and down the steep steps to get our suitcases and four Trader Joe bags up to the cabin.

Dylan quickly starts to put everything away into the refrigerator, pulling out the salad fixings to make something for our lunch. We drove up early in the morning so we could have a whole day here. I quickly text the owner, tell him that everything's great, that we love it, and that I'll be in touch later if we need anything. Our vacation is now ready to begin. We eat lunch on the porch looking out at the lake below, and after a tasty lunch of arugula salad with poached eggs, a side of strawberries, and Trader Joe's cucumber dill dressing for me and Caesar for Dylan.

We change into our bathing suits, grab our towels, put on flip-flops, and head down to the beach. The sand is soft, yellow, and we're the only ones here. I lay out my towel, grab my iPad, and begin to sunbathe.

"Aren't you coming in?" Dylan asks.

"I've got to warm up a little bit, but you go."

He pulls off his shirt and heads down to the water dipping his toes in and then turning back to me. "It's amazing, the perfect temperature, come on in. I can see all the way to the bottom."

I've always loved swimming in lakes. There's something peaceful about them that's so different than battling the waves of the ocean. They can be muddy bottomed or perfectly clear, but I love the stillness of the water. Something about it puts me completely at ease.

Quail Lake was formed by the snow that falls here in the winters and the scattered rainfall the rest of the year, so the shoreline varies a lot depending on how much of a drought Southern California is having. The shoreline has been decreasing steadily, but last winter we got a lot of snow so it was replenished and it's almost back to where it was originally.

I get up from my towel and take a few barefoot steps to the edge of the water. The sand is soft under my feet, but the sand disappears a couple of feet under the water and the lake bed itself is rocky until you get out deeper where the silt and vegetation take over.

Dylan is about knee-deep in, waves to me, and gives me a wide smile. Something about swimming in the lake, something about being here makes me feel like a child at camp, the carefree time that summers represent in youth. They're fleeting and you have to make sure you savor each moment.

Dylan's burns are still quite visible, especially in the bright afternoon sunlight, but he doesn't seem bothered by them and I'm not either. His scarring is getting better, but I wonder if they'll ever go away completely.

Scar tissue is different from regular skin; it doesn't pain the same, doesn't heal the same way, and it's thicker. I don't mind it of course. I still love Dylan the same, unconditionally, but I just don't want him to feel strange about it, bad about himself for no reason.

I wade into the water, Dylan takes a few steps further out and then dives in. When he comes out, he waves; he switches his hair to one side with one swoop, his eyes glistening in the sunlight. A smile lights up his whole face and I realize that this is the man that I want to spend the rest of my life with.

"Come in. What's taking you so long?" he yells and waves to me.

I slowly put one foot in front of the other. The water is not cold, far from it, but it's a little chilled and I always take a long time and torture myself when entering any cool body of water. As my legs slowly go numb, and it spreads up to my waist, I force myself to put my shoulders under and let out a little yelp as I do.

"Ah, that feels good." I smile. Dylan pulls me into his arms and gives me a kiss. Our mouths touch and when he pulls away, I pull closer and kiss him back.

"I missed you," he says.

"Me, too."

He tugs at the top of my swimsuit and with one pull of the string the top part of the one-piece falls down.

"What are you doing?" I laugh, loving the feeling of the freedom of my naked body against the water. I look around to make sure that no one is around. It's Thursday, midday, and we seem to be the only ones here.

Still, I try to pull my top up to tie it again, and he pulls me close and feels all around and flips me around and kisses me again. The bottom of my hair has fallen into the water, even though I hadn't planned on getting it wet, but I like it that way. It feels good on my neck and body. Then I turn around, but when he reaches over to tug at my bathing suit again, I push and splash him, a wave of water washes over him and he just cracks up laughing.

"Don't start a war you can't finish."

A tsunami hits me in my face, drenching every strand of my hair. I give up trying to stay dry, wipe my eyes, and then lie down on my back and float peacefully, looking at the bright blue sky with a few little puffs of clouds out in the distance. As I float under the pine trees, I listen to the songs of birds, chirping away, one trying to outdo the other, and I realize that there's no more perfect place to be than right here, right now.

Of course, Dylan splashes me again, breaking the reverie and I can't let him get away with it. I tackle him, push him under the water, and he does the same to me. We come up for air laughing. Our bodies are wrapped around one another, feeling like teenagers, as opposed to thirty-somethings.

"I've always wanted to go to camp," I say as we struggle for breath and call a temporary truce.

"Oh, yeah?"

"Yes. Someplace like this, you know, *away*."

"Your dad never signed you up?" Dylan asks.

"No, I don't even know if it occurred to him. By the time I got to high school, I was too cool for something like this, but secretly I always wanted to go to sleep away camp, stay in a cabin with like, four girlfriends. We would talk about boys, do arts and crafts, and be kids."

"Yes, it was great."

"Don't tell me you did that."

"Yes. Three summers in a row starting sixth grade, and then I was a camp counselor."

"Oh my God. How was it?" I ask.

"As amazing as they show in movies, minus the drama. I mean, there was a little bit of drama, who liked who, trying to hook up with the girls and trying not to step on your friends' toes if they liked them and you liked them, too, but other than that, it was just awesome. My parents were having a bit of trouble then, arguing a lot, talking about divorce. It was nice to have this place to go to, and when I got to be the camp counselor it was just ultimate freedom. I was the one who was in charge, making the rules, helping the younger kids, and I always thought it would be fun to open a camp when I got older to capture that mood and create those memories for other kids."

"Wow. I had no idea about this, about you, Dylan."

"Well, we've been dating for a little bit, but you don't know everything."

"Still, I'm really surprised."

"When you have good experiences, you want to give back, you want to create that for someone else."

"Is that something you seriously considered?"

He nods a little bit. "Yes, I never had the startup money. It's expensive, insurance, the place, especially California in particular. It's just a lot to rent the space, and I was, what, detective? In San Francisco I could barely pay the rent, and then a firefighter, worse hours, better conditions until you get burned alive that is, but still no money to really do something like this."

"Yeah, I get it," I say.

"You want to drive around? Want to see if there's a camp like that here? Maybe look it up online?"

"They don't actually let you join as an adult. You know that, right?" he jokes, tilting his head.

I push him under the water again. I wait for him to come up and he doesn't. I wait a few more beats and then something grabs onto my ankles and pulls me down. I let out a scream, right before my mouth is muffled by the water.

When he lets go, I start to laugh, and that's when I actually choke.

"Okay, a few deep breaths," he keeps saying as I continue to cough. "Sorry, I didn't realize I was going to actually drown you."

"You didn't, you didn't," I say when I'm finally able to catch my breath. "Just kind of went into the wrong pipe."

"Who knows, maybe it's something that we'll be able to do with our kids," he says, after a long pause. "Even if I don't start a camp, we should definitely send them to one."

"Our kids?"

He nods. "Yes. You want to have kids, right?"

I bite my lower lip. My answer to that question was always no, but, with him posing it, it suddenly becomes a maybe.

"You'd be a great mom. I know that you think that you wouldn't. You didn't have an example and your dad wasn't really that involved, but you would be, I know it. You're fun, you're easygoing. You don't worry about things that don't matter. What more could a kid want?"

He leaves that thought hanging in the air as he pushes me under again. I take a big gulp of water and spit it at him. When I come up for air, we both laugh and the birds above our heads chirp and the sun continues to shine.

For a little while there, everything is as happy as it could be.

3

CHARLOTTE

While Dylan and I sit around on the porch eating the s'mores that we made in the small fire pit, I tell him how I used to feel about summers.

It felt like I would wait for them forever, but they would be gone in an instant. I just count down the days backward until finally, it was summertime.

I would want to seize the days, but after a week of being lazy, you kind of fall into this trap of doing nothing.

I spent most summers in a public pool. The days that it rained, I felt like I got cheated because that was one less day of pool time that I could've enjoyed.

"Yes, I spent a lot of time in camps and at a lake just like this one, but in Northern California," Dylan says.

"Big sequoias. Fun times. I made some good friends. Most of them work in the tech industry now, making a lot more money than I do."

"Do you ever regret going into police work?"

"Yes, all the time. So, I don't do it anymore."

"I know about your partner, but what about everything else?"

"I don't love it, Charlotte. I mean, I know you enjoy your job, I know you don't complain about it, but I never felt that way. I went into it because my brother was missing and I thought it was something that I could do to help, if only I knew more about the process. Well, I realized that the investigators were telling me the truth and until more evidence comes in, I'll never know what happened to him."

He brings up his missing brother in the casual kind of way that he has in the past, but I know that it gives him a lot of pain.

Dylan's brother disappeared as an adult and those are the hardest people to find, mostly because investigators and law enforcement agencies feel in some cases that adults can go missing if they want to, and this is correct in some ways.

They don't have to reply to their parents or their siblings requests to be in touch.

They don't have to tell them what's going on.

They don't need updates.

It's their right to disappear.

That's a very different case from what happened to Kelsey, my friend, who went missing when she was thirteen years old.

I've told Dylan about it, the case, and he occasionally brings it up.

"You still in touch with her?"

"Yes, we've been texting back and forth. It's kind of fun having this friend from the past."

"That's good to hear," he says. "You have any idea why the DNA doesn't match?"

"No." I shake my head. "No clue. I need to get her parents' DNA but, of course, the police up there aren't willing to share it. I reached out to them, told them about the predicament, and they think that if the DNA doesn't match, then it's not her."

"You believe that it is?"

"I know it is. I saw her in the flesh. She's Kelsey Hall. I mean, she looks a little different, but it's her."

"What about the memories? She doesn't have that many, right?"

"Yes, that's true, but she remembers me and a lot of details from that night. We talked about it."

"What are your plans?"

"Next time I can squeeze some time off, I'm going to go up to Seattle where her parents live, meet up with them, talk to them, ask them for their DNA to see if maybe we can match it up."

"And what if they say no?"

"If they say no, that's a bigger problem." I shrug.

I reach into the bag of marshmallows and pop one into my mouth without bothering to melt it.

Dylan looks at me like I'm a barbarian.

He's the kind of person who takes his time roasting it, slowly turning it and making sure that it doesn't get burned and it's equally toasted on all sides. Me, I'll torch it, bite into it, wait for the gooey part in the middle to come out, and chew through the cold bits on the outside.

If there were a metaphor for our different personalities, our approach to marshmallow-toasting would be it.

I take a Hershey square and pop that in my mouth.

"You know it tastes better if it's all together, right? You know that, right?"

"Yes, but it tastes pretty good as individual ingredients as well."

"Yes, but the whole point of toasting marshmallows and making s'mores is the experience."

"Well, you were doing your part and taking forever, and I didn't want to wait."

I point to the small tabletop, marshmallow fire pit that we're sharing.

Since California is in a perpetual drought, there're no big fire pits allowed anywhere near the forest, so this is the best we can do.

"What do you think about a little skinny-dipping?"

"What?"

The lake is all ours, and the moon's about to come out.

"Come on, it'll be fun."

"You mean, no bathing suit?"

"No."

He shakes his head and grabs my hand.

He puts the metal cap on top of the fire pit, and I let him drag me down to the lake.

There's a little breeze coming off the water.

It tosses my hair from side to side, and I take off my flip-flops and step into the water.

Dylan's way ahead of me.

He pulls off his shirt and then unbuckles his shorts.

"You're really going to go skinny-dipping?"

"Yes. Do you see anyone out here?"

"What about all of those houses with the lights on? They could see you."

"Not really. We have no lights on and there're no lights on around here. The only ones who will see us are the fish. Come on, take off your clothes."

He walks back out and when I hesitate, he pulls off my tank top.

I'm not wearing a bra and he exposes me to the breeze, pulling down my shorts.

He grabs my hand again and pulls me into the water.

It feels cool as I descend under, my hair floating briefly on top before sinking down.

Dylan walks over and kisses me, cradling my head in his hands.

"I love you," he whispers. "I love you more than --"

He hesitates. For a second, I wonder if he's thinking about saying 'more than I've loved anyone' and then not wanting to tell a lie.

He frowns slightly.

Dylan was married for a while, many years ago, and his wife tragically died in a car accident.

We haven't talked about her much, just a little, and I'm the first serious relationship that he's been in since.

"I love you to the moon. I love you more than anything, and I want you to know that you complete me," he whispers.

He kisses me again.

"What does that mean? To you, I mean?" I ask, pulling away. "I'm not trying to be smart or clever but I'm just seriously asking you the question."

"Until we met, I didn't realize how lost I was, how confused my life was. It feels like it makes sense with you in it, and I just want you to know that because I'm planning to be in your life for a long time."

I kiss him back.

"Look, you complete me, too," I whisper. "And I love you."

We lose ourselves in our bodies, in the water around us.

He feels me everywhere and our hands and legs intertwine with one another.

We kiss underwater and we kiss above the water under the moonlight, and the world has never made more sense than it does at this very moment.

Then we drag ourselves to the shore and into bed.

We make love on the sheets, not caring that they're getting drenched with our wet bodies.

I sleep a long time, well into the morning, and the thing that wakes me is the smell of coffee coming from the kitchen and the aroma of eggs cooking on a skillet.

4

SARAH

Sarah's heart started pounding as soon as she turned to walk to the end of the dock. It was so unlike her, but there was no one else around, and the fact that they were the only two up would be a conversation starter, more of an opening than she'd had in two weeks.

Dominic sat on the edge of the dock in his Camp Quail Lake T-shirt with two recently heated frozen waffles next to him. He took a bite of one and then broke off little crumbs to feed the ducks who'd started gathering below him. He gave her a slight nod when he heard her walking down the dock. He didn't turn around but didn't act like she was a nuisance either, which she appreciated.

"What are you doing up?" Sarah asked, crossing her arms and widening her stance, hunching herself over a little more and leaning closer to him, casting a wide shadow.

Dominic looked up at her, his eyes squinted, "Here, come sit down. I can't see a thing."

She smiled to herself at the invitation but wondered if he actually wanted her to sit down or the sun was just too bright to look at.

"Haven't been to bed yet," Dominic said. "How about you?"

"I'm an early riser. Can't sleep past five thirty."

"Seriously? You must not go to sleep late enough."

He shrugged.

The two of them looked out at the crystal-clear water. There was a distinct scent of summer that morning. The sun was starting to warm up the lake, warm up their shoulders, and as it evaporated the dew on the grass, everything seemed to come alive and become more lush.

SARAH PRESSED her palms together and felt the sweat on them. It wasn't that warm yet, the sweat was from her nerves. This is the most that she had talked to Dominic in weeks, except for the one time she'd helped him look for the watch that he'd lost somewhere in the woods the first week of camp. That was the most exhilarating afternoon of her life so far, and the fact that they couldn't find it made it ever so much more exciting.

"Hey, did you ever find that watch of yours?" she asked, trying to be as casual as possible.

"No, someone must have snagged it."

"That's too bad," she said.

"Yes, my mom gave it to me for Christmas a couple of years ago. It wasn't very expensive or anything like that, more sentimental, you know?"

"Wow, you have sentimental things attached your mom?" The words had just slipped out without her realizing it.

He turned to look at her. "Of course. You don't?"

"Hardly." She shrugged. "My parents are like ships passing in the night. They're hardly around, and when they are, they just act like I'm some decoration, a very expensive token to toss back and forth and fight over. Their divorce lasted for three years and neither of them cared how it hurt me to testify and give all those depositions about where I did and didn't want to live, et cetera, et cetera."

She rolled her eyes and let out a deep sigh.

"Sorry, I don't mean to put all that crap on you," she added, suddenly realizing that she had let her personality escape for a moment, her true personality.

Here she was trying to be her bubbly, friendly self that she thought would make Dominic most likely to be interested in her, and then she made a mistake, let the truth slip out.

"I'm really sorry about that." Dominic shrugged, his shoulders moving slowly up and down. His sympathy made Sarah fall for him even more.

"So, you never said, why are you out here?" she asked, realizing that her heart was starting to beat faster and faster out of her chest. If she had waited for a little more, it might escape completely.

"Okay. Let me tell you, but promise not to laugh, okay?"

She nodded and tilted her head. "I'll keep your secret, I promise."

Dominic said with a deep sigh, another one that made him even more attractive somehow.

"My girlfriend just broke up with me last night. She wrote me a 'Dear John' letter."

SARAH HAD no idea what a "Dear John" letter was, and neither did Dominic. Not really. She knew vaguely that it was somehow connected to the letters that men who were at war received from their girlfriends when they couldn't put up with the distance anymore, and that was why they called it that.

"We only really saw each other at camp. We somehow managed to hold onto this relationship for a year with more than our share of long-distance fights," he said, slouching his shoulders and hanging his head, his hair falling in his face.

"I was just trying to hold on until we finally got back to camp to make it all worth it, but she couldn't."

"She goes here?" Sarah asked.

He nodded. "We were on and off together for a bit."

"How did I not know this?" she asked.

"We tried to keep it a secret. It was my idea more than hers. She thought that I was embarrassed about her. She thought that I didn't want to be with her, but I did. I was just conflicted."

Sarah didn't quite understand what he was talking about, but Dominic kept going in circles talking to her, but largely at her.

"Who's your girlfriend?" Sarah asked, leaning back, propping herself up on the edge of the dock with her feet hanging into the water. The cool water felt good against the bottom of her feet. She moved them around more to fidget than anything else.

Dominic bent over even more, pushing his fingers into the water, scooping it up in his palm. For a second, she thought that maybe he was going to drink, but instead he tossed it into his hair and looked up at her, his eyes twinkling. If she hadn't slept a wink last night, she'd look wrecked, exhausted, spent, but not him.

His demeanor and his charm were completely effortless, and that was what made her fall in love with him even more. She felt pathetic, sad, lost here. She had been pining for him for so long and he'd had a girlfriend all this time. A girl who was at camp with them no less, not someone from back home. How pathetic? How ridiculous?

"Misty Copeland," Dominic said, tilting his head to the side, the sun glistening off the water creating a mosaic around his face. Sarah knew exactly who Misty Copeland was. Tall, statuesque blonde with long hair, longer nails, and a tomboy personality that made her that cool girl that everyone wanted to be.

Her skin was perfect. Her tan was golden. Her eyes twinkled when she smiled. She had a way of making you feel you were the only one she was talking to and the only one who mattered. The thing that Sarah hated most about Misty was how nice she was to everyone. She stopped the bullies from being mean to the younger kids. She befriended the friendless. She smiled at everyone and tried to make the days here as pleasant as possible. She was the camp counselor that everyone wanted to have.

"Why didn't you want to say that you two were dating?" Sarah asked. "She's gorgeous, I'd probably want to scream it from the rooftops."

"I have a whole thing with labels and relationships."

"You wanted to date her, but pretend you were single and hang out with other girls as well?" Sarah furrowed her brow. Her desire for him suddenly started to evaporate. Was he a mean guy after all?

"Look, everybody loves Misty, but she isn't as perfect as you all think she is."

"Maybe not. Nobody is," Sarah said. "But still, it's a crappy move to hide your relationship, right?"

"She said she wanted it that way," Dominic said, "at first. Listen, I don't need a lecture. It's hard to explain how I felt at the time."

"Yes, I understand. It's your business." Sarah nodded and looked out into the distance.

If he couldn't deal with Misty being his girlfriend, there was no way that he'd be into Sarah.

"I don't know for sure, but I think Misty met someone about a month ago," he finally admitted. "She got distant and wouldn't call me as much, wouldn't email. She said it was because of our relationship, but who knows? Finally, she wrote me that letter by hand. She could have emailed it. I would've known right away, but she mailed it out."

"The 'Dear John' letter?" Sarah asked.

He nodded.

"She told me that she couldn't do this long distance anymore, but we weren't going to. We were going to be together in a week for the whole summer."

"Have you talked to her since?"

"No." Dominic shook his head. "I can't deal with it. I have seen her, but we didn't even acknowledge each other."

Sarah had never had a relationship, but she had read about plenty of them, and she knew that things were very complicated. Things that could seem very simple and happy on the outside could be fractious and difficult on the inside. Relationships seemed to be stratified into all these layers. Feelings, responses to feelings, interactions. They were never one thing, they were always another. Sometimes you moved through a tangled briar patch in the dark.

"Well, I hope that you can make it right," she said after a little while.

"No, we can't." He shook his head. "I'm here just processing it all. I thought I was over it, but I found the letter again and reread it."

"I think you need to speak to her," Sarah suggested. "The way you are talking to me now. Tell her about your feelings. That's the only thing she wants to hear," Sarah insisted. "So many things happen from people miscommunicating how they feel, misunderstanding how someone else felt, their motivations. Obviously, we're not all in control of and in full knowledge of why we do the things we do, but it's worth a try. Don't you think?"

"I don't know. She told me she didn't want to be with me. I don't want to go groveling back."

"You're not groveling," Sarah insisted. "You're asking for clarification."

"She's with someone else, Sarah, don't you get it? Oh, yes. I forgot. You've never been with anyone."

Sarah recoiled. The meanness came out of nowhere and it hurt her to her soul.

"I'm sorry. I didn't mean to say that."

56

A wave of emotion came over her and tears started to come out of her eyes.

She rose up to her feet. He grabbed her hand, but she pulled away.

"Get away from me," she snapped.

"Sarah, please. I'm sorry. You have to forgive me. I know you were just trying to help and I'm being an asshole."

"Yes, you are."

He grabbed her hand again and pulled her close. "Please don't leave. I need you," he whispered.

She was being held by him in a hug, something that she had dreamed of for a long time, but never thought that it would come like this. Why could he only say this to her after he had hurt her? Is this what he was like? Full of anger and meanness?

She couldn't be sure, but she stayed there anyway, and he held her for a while. She listened to the fast beat of his heart as it slowed down ever so slightly with each breath.

5

CHARLOTTE

The following morning I go out on an early run, crawling out of bed and forcing myself outside to get some blood flowing through my body. Dylan is still asleep but I like this time to myself. It's not particularly early anymore, but it's still morning to me. The water is calling my name but I won't let myself go in for a dip without first running at least a mile and a half.

The blue sky and the fresh mountain air do their best to jolt my sleepy state into life without caffeine. I put on a podcast and begin to move, putting one foot in front of the other until it starts to resemble something of a jog.

Rushing along the busy lakeshore, I look straight ahead hoping that no drivers swerve into me by accident. I lose myself in the podcast hosts' gaggle and laughter over nothing in particular until someone becomes almost impossible to miss.

"Help! Help!" she yells, waving her arms at me.

When our eyes meet, I realize that she's screaming for me to come and I sprint toward her over the rocky shore, letting the tall weeds lash against my shins.

As soon as she sees me heading toward her, she lets her arms drop and looks down at something on the ground. Following her gaze, I see a body.

"I found a girl. She's dead," the woman says when I get close. I lean over to confirm that she has no pulse, pausing for a moment to watch as the water brushes up and over her head, almost cradling her.

"Aren't you going to do anything?" the woman asks me in an accusatory manner.

"She's deceased, ma'am," I say, gathering my breath.

"No, she can't be."

The woman about a decade older than I am seems to be going through a kind of cognitive dissonance. She's the one who first told me that this girl was dead but now can't seem to believe it to be true. She takes a few steps away from me and sits down on a large boulder, pushing her knees up to her chest and wrapping her arms around them, bearing her head.

I give her a few moments and take a look around. There's a camera slung around the woman's back. An expensive kind. Not just the phone. She's dressed in capri pants and an oversized button-down shirt, casual. She had come out here to what, exactly? Take pictures? Not exercise, for certain. Maybe a walk? When she appears to gather herself a little bit, I ask her for her name.

Her name is Cindy Morales and she is an amateur photographer, an attorney by trade. She's here for the weekend, taking pictures of birds and nature.

"I was planning on coming out at daybreak, but I slept in. Had a little too much wine last night. I'm going through a breakup."

"Sorry about that," I say, reflexively.

She shrugs. "I was just walking around taking pictures, saw a hawk and an eagle, and then I just stumbled upon her. I wasn't looking down and I tripped over her, actually. At first, I thought it was a doll or something like that. I've never seen a dead body before. Not out like this."

"That must have been really scary," I say. She nods, looking away from the dead girl as much as possible, even turning her body away to face me.

"Why are you so calm?" she asks. "Aren't you going to call the police?"

"Actually, I am the police."

I report the dead body soon after. Gavin Skeeter is the first one to show up. I had met him earlier when I worked a case up here not too long ago and he gives me a brief hug and says that one of these days we should actually catch up, but not over a corpse. I agree that that would be a good idea and one that I'd really appreciate.

Once the scene is cordoned off, he takes Cindy's statement and asks me for mine. I confirm what Cindy told me and tell him that the only thing I did was check her pulse to make sure that she was indeed dead but, as far as I know, neither of us have touched the body, other than that. I'm not a crime scene investigator, but by the looks of it, she does not look like she's been here very long. Her body's cool to the touch but hasn't started decomposing yet. Given the rising temperature, it would start much faster than if this were wintertime.

She's lying face up on the edge of the water, her head partially submerged. There are bruises all over her body and a big gash on the top of her head.

"I don't see any other blood around here. Nothing obvious anyway. If there had been a tussle and she was hit by a rock, then there would've been more blood all over these smooth rocks over here," I point out.

"What are you saying?" Gavin asks.

He's a rookie, not first year on the job, but not very experienced. This town doesn't usually have a lot of murders or suspicious deaths to investigate and he's eager to learn how to do things right.

"There are a lot of bruises on her," I say. "Maybe she was even strangled." I point to her neck where the bruises have become quite prominent. "Her face has a lot of scrapes as well."

"We will need to get an autopsy, of course, to see if there are contusions or damage to her skull to determine what could have happened. So far, I don't see any stab or bullet wounds, so most likely asphyxiation or blunt force trauma," I point out. "If the struggle and the death occurred here, I just suspect that there would be more evidence."

"What do you mean by that?" Gavin asks, writing everything I'm saying carefully in his notebook.

I walk around with my phone, making more notes and he follows.

"Recording your thoughts is a better way to go?" he asks.

"Yes, especially in scenes like this; you can just record what you see, initial impressions and then go through it for the report."

"What makes you think that it didn't happen here?"

"There seems to be a lot of bodily harm," I point out. "Where's the evidence of what could have happened? Where's the proof that-- Where's the blood, where's evidence of the tussle, the fight? It would be all over these rocks. I don't know for sure, of course, but it was something that we would need to find proof of. You know what I mean?"

He nods. I walk around the body some more. Long red hair, pale face, freckles, a little bit of makeup that got smeared around the eyes from tears. She's dressed in shorts and a tank top. When I look closer at the bruising around her arms, I notice that all is not what it seems.

"There are cuts here." I point to Gavin. "Do you see? They have healed. You see the white bumps around her forearms and on the inside of her thighs? Small little cuts in a particular pattern. One line after another, those have healed. Those are from a while ago."

"Oh my God. Do you think that someone had kept her and was abusing her?"

I shake my head.

"That's one possibility, of course. We'll see if she's from here or if there's somebody else or perhaps then yes, but it's unlikely that abuse cuts would be so perfect, so similar as if they were done with the exact same blade all the time. Plus, they're quite small."

He nods his head. "What do you think it is?"

"I think she had been hurting herself for a little while. She's a teenage girl. It's not completely out of the realm of possibility."

"What do you mean she has been hurting herself?"

"When they take her body and do the autopsy, they'll check if her weapon is on her, if this little blade, maybe a razor blade is on her somewhere."

"Why would she do that?"

"To let out pain, to deal with anxiety, deal with a world that's too much."

"You know a lot about this," Gavin asks and then looks at my arms and legs.

I shake my head.

He recoils right away. "Sorry, I didn't mean to pry. This is way too personal."

"No, I expect nothing else from a good investigator." I smile. "I'm glad you looked and you made the connection, but no, I've never cut myself, but I know people who did. I've also seen it on the job a few times."

"Wow, that sucks."

"I think there's only one thing that's unusual," I point out. "If she were indeed cutting herself, she would make sure that she was wearing long sleeves, long pants. These scars are visible, something that the person is gravely ashamed of doing. She is wearing a T-shirt and shorts. Why? I don't know."

I call Dylan and fill him in about my morning this far. He asks how long I'm going to be, and I tell him, "I really don't know. I don't want to leave Gavin alone, but the crime scene investigator should be here soon, and they will prep the body, collect evidence, and take it away. Then I should be free. Couple of hours maybe," I add. "Why don't you get breakfast, and then we'll meet up for lunch?"

He doesn't say much but I can tell that he's mildly annoyed, but I don't pay attention. I don't apologize either. This is my job, and I have to make sure it's done right while it's on my watch.

6

CHARLOTTE

I t takes the CSI people a bit longer than I expected to come here, and I have to make a couple more excuses to Dylan. Eventually, he just gives up and comes up to visit us. I introduce him to Gavin. I tell Gavin that I really have to go, but that he can handle this himself. He looks lost. He shakes his head no and pulls me aside.

"I don't think I can do this by myself," he says. "Everybody's off this weekend and you know that we need to do interviews and all that stuff as soon as possible in order to find out what has happened."

"What about your boss?" I ask.

"He's out, too. It's a very slim force when everyone is here. I have to call Lieutenant Soderman to see if they can send someone else up. Can you just wait until then?"

I bite my lower lip.

"Why don't I get on the call with you?" I ask, begrudgingly.

I know Lieutenant Soderman well enough to know that he doesn't like to send people to deal with problems when a perfectly fine detective like me is available. He probably wouldn't care. The lieutenant answers on the second ring and I fill him in about what has happened.

"Is no one available up there?" he asks.

"No, I'm the only one up here right now. The local lieutenant is taking care of a family emergency. It was supposed to be a quiet weekend."

"Yes, I can see that," Lieutenant Soderman says, and I can hear him tapping his finger on the table. "I don't see any other way around it, Charlotte. I mean, I know you're on a break, but you're up there anyway. Maybe you can take some time and interview some people. Try to find out if this girl is at least from the area. Gavin's a deputy and inexperienced even for that. This is above his pay grade."

I swallow hard. I know this is the only way to do it, but I still am not going to be happy about it. "Yes, okay. I'll help him find out who the victim is, who might have done this."

"Good. Okay. Keep me updated."

I take a deep breath as I turn to face Dylan. He knows that things are going to be different on this trip despite my best efforts, without me even having to tell him. But he still tries to find a way around the inevitable.

"What about Will?" he asks. "Can't he do this?"

I shake my head no. "Will is out for good. The judge declared a mistrial because the evidence they collected against Erin's husband's law partner was fruit of a poisoned tree and therefore it's all tainted."

"So, they're just going to let that guy go who killed two people or rather three since she was pregnant?"

"Yes, for now. They're going to try to build another case somehow, but the judge didn't buy the inevitable discovery argument."

"What about Will himself?" Dylan asks.

"He's probably going to lose his badge. Internal Affairs is investigating. But what he did is highly improper. We just can't have a relationship with the primary suspect in a murder case you're investigating."

We're out of earshot from Gavin. I whisper under my breath to Dylan that Lieutenant Soderman doesn't want me to say a thing about me knowing about any of it. I'm going to be interviewed as well, but he doesn't want to lose two good detectives over this. Especially since it's clear that someone else had done it.

"What about all the other charges against that guy?" Dylan asks. "I mean, it wasn't just the murder, kidnapping, all that stuff."

"Yes." I nod. "That's the angle that I'm hoping they're going to take. Push for prosecuting the things that he did afterward. Maybe they can't get him on murder, but they can get him on everything else including tax evasion, who knows? The IRS got Al Capone. Hopefully they can get him."

Our conversation trails and meanders mostly because neither of us want to talk about what this means for our weekend.

"I'm going to have to do a lot of interviews. I want Gavin to take the lead, do a lot of the actual investigation so I can have some time off, but he needs my help. There's no way around it."

"Charlotte!" Gavin yells. "Look." He points to a tag that falls out of the victim's pocket when they lift her up. It says Camp Quail Lake. "That's a lead, right?" he asks.

I nod. "Yes, that's a big lead. That's the first place we have to go."

7

CHARLOTTE

Gavin and I drive into Camp Quail Lake later that afternoon. It's abuzz with activity. Children are yelling, having fun by the dock. Others are in canoes racing each other across the lake. There's a small swimming area with campers running, splashing, lounging, and joking around. There's a big wooden sign with the words Camp Quail Lake carved into it. The peeling paint and the haphazard axe carving gives it an air of authenticity.

The dirt road is long and winding and we drive past a larger cabin that says "Administration" on the front. Gavin is about to pull over, but I tell him to keep going.

"I want to take a look around, just briefly," I say.

We drive down the dirt road to a group of wooden cabins on the left, designated girls, and ones across the street, designated boys.

There are picnic tables with awnings where other campers are doing arts and crafts, and in general, living their best summer lives. A place like this was a dream of mine growing up, a place I could only imagine going to, memorialized in numerous movies and TV shows, filled with nostalgia, horror, and everything in between.

It was a place that I used to imagine as an eleven-year-old, where I would have my first crush, my first kiss, my first whatever. Something about being in an enclosed place with kids your own age, and a few older ones who were like older brothers and sisters seemed like the perfect combination for a summer romance or the flowering of a beautiful friendship.

I don't know how far from reality my pre-adolescent imagination was, but we're about to find out. We make a loop around and park in front of the administration cabin. A plump man in shorts and a branded Quail Lake T-shirt comes out and introduces himself as Dr. Abbott, the director of the camp. He's tan with rounded cheeks, the kind that are used to smiling most of the time. Unfortunately, today he meets me with a grave expression on his face.

We had called earlier, gave a description of the girl who we'd found, and he confirmed that she had not reported to her morning or afternoon activities.

"Thank you so much for coming out," Dr. Abbott says, shaking my hand feverishly and looking quite distraught.

He ushers both of us into his office, a small room in the larger cabin, the rest of which consist of a few other offices and is connected to the dining hall and the kitchen. He pulls out a plastic folding chair for one of us to use. Gavin offers me the plush fabric one across from Dr. Abbott's desk.

"Thank you again so much for coming out. Just overcome with disbelief. I can't imagine that it's actually her."

"Do you have any pictures or anything we can use to confirm her identity before we call her parents?"

"Yes, of course." He nods, opens his laptop, and pulls up the records on all the campers. "She's one of our counselors. She's always been so good and reliable. I don't know how this could have happened."

"How does it work when you're a counselor?" I ask.

"Well, you have a lot more leeway. Of course, we rely on their bunkmates to make sure that we know that they're in for the night and everyone is supposed to report if something unusual has happened or if someone is missing."

"There was no report like this made?"

"No." He shakes his head. "Not at all."

"What about this morning?"

"Well, it's hard to tell. After you called, I made the rounds and found out that she was supposed to be in art and crafts in the afternoon, and she wasn't there. She was also supposed to be helping with the canoes, but she was a floater today."

"Meaning?" I ask for clarification.

"If somebody weren't feeling well or needed a break, she would be called, but it wasn't regular duty. When she didn't show up, I guess no one thought anything of it."

"So, she was a substitute?"

"Yes, in a way. Sometimes our counselors get a little overwhelmed. They need a break in the middle of the day. We have others who have a half-day off that are on call and so they pick up the slack. We found that this works best to give everyone the time and space they need, as long as no one is abusing the system."

"Was anyone abusing the system as far as you could tell?"

"No, not this summer. We haven't had any issues. We have such a great set of counselors. All of them have been with us for years as campers. That's who we prefer to hire. They're friends. They think of the smaller kids as their little brothers and sisters. They're very caring."

Suddenly, Dr. Abbott gets overwhelmed. I can see that he's close to tears, but he takes a few deep breaths to calm himself and a tight smile returns to his face.

"Okay, here it is," he says, pointing to the screen.

He turns it toward us and I see a smiling redhead beaming from ear to ear, excited for eight weeks of summer fun. The dark auburn hair that I saw earlier floating in the lake is really a bright reddish color, but the freckles on her face are spot on.

I had stared at that face all morning, and though we have to call her parents or next of kin for the formal identification, Gavin and I exchange looks and we both know that unfortunately, the dead body belongs to Sarah Dunn of Pasadena, California.

8

CHARLOTTE

Dr. Abbott offers to bring Sarah's other three bunkmates to speak to us in one place, but I'd rather catch them by surprise, pull them aside and get their initial impressions. It's not procedure to speak to them at the same time, and I don't want them putting their stories together. Luckily, they're working three different positions, and I ask Dr. Abbott for help with pulling them away from their duties without arousing too much suspicion about who we are or what we're doing here. The rumor mill that the camp will likely become has to be contained so that Sarah's parents can be notified appropriately.

Sarah was murdered somewhere in Quail Lake, of that I'm certain. She was present in her bunk last night. There's no use in wasting time waiting for her parents to be notified, as they likely had nothing to do with this untimely passing. Dr. Abbott agrees with our strategy, and we head out to talk to Bennett Olsen first.

On the way over, I debate with myself how many details I can give her and decide to keep her in the dark for now. We find her by a lifeguard station and Dr. Abbott has her switch with a girl who's taking a break and talk to us a little bit to the side away from the campers. Bennett is a broad-shouldered, fit, or rather very strong-looking woman who's wearing a bracelet with the Harvard University logo on it. I introduce myself and Gavin and ask her about the last time that she had seen her bunkmate, Sarah.

Bennett looks surprised. She's dressed in black shorts and an oversized Camp Quail Lake T-shirt with a name tag. Her curly brown hair is pulled up into a ponytail and hidden under a baseball cap. Her face is flushed from sitting in the sun as she pulls off her sporty sunglasses to look me straight in the eye.

"I saw her last night. She definitely went to bed with everyone else."

"Was she there this morning?"

"Yes, she was." She nods. "The day before she went wandering around. Said she couldn't sleep and woke up early, but then today she woke up with the rest of us."

"Do you usually have breakfast together?" I ask.

"No. Sometimes, but she was running late. She wanted to take a shower when there's really no point."

"There's no point in taking a shower?" I ask.

Bennett shifts her weight from one foot to another.

"I guess you can, but being a counselor is sweaty work, especially in the heat and all. Usually everyone showers at the end of the day, but she said she wanted to wash her hair. We all went to the dining hall to have breakfast."

"Did you see her after that?"

"No." She shakes her head.

"Okay." I nod. "Can you tell me anything else about her? What was your relationship like?"

"We're friends. We've known each other forever."

"What's her relationship like with your roommates?"

"Good. We're like sisters. We've been coming here for years. First as campers, then counselors. I mean, we don't really have a lot in common, but we have this history, and it seems to be enough."

"It seems to be enough?" I ask. Bennett shrugs.

"I wouldn't say that I would be friends with everyone that I'm roommates with if I hadn't met them at camp, you know? But the history is worth something. We're all going to go to college, meet new people, start our lives, but we have this past, this fun time at Quail Lake."

"What about Sarah? Do you think she was having a good time here?"

"Of course. This place is magical."

"What were her plans for the future?"

"I don't know. Her mom is expecting her to go to USC, but I don't know if that'll happen."

"Oh, yes? Why not?"

"She said that she doesn't even want to apply. Her parents are both legacies. Her mom thinks that she should be in her old sorority. She'll meet the right guy in a fraternity, but that's exactly where her mom met her dad, and it didn't exactly work out."

"What school would you think would be a good fit for her? Is she more artsy? Does she like science?"

"Why don't you just ask her yourself?" Bennett asks, shrugging her shoulders, and looking away from me for a moment. When our eyes meet again, I see her composure break a little. The cool girl suddenly disappears just a little bit. She narrows her eyes and stares at me.

"Something happened to Sarah. Is that why you're asking all these questions?"

Being asked point-blank, I hesitate. You're supposed to tell the next of kin first, prior to anyone else, but this situation is complicated by the fact that they're not answering their phones and it's probably going to take them a long time to come up here and identify the body.

"We found her murdered," Gavin says.

I glare at him, unable to believe that I heard what I think I heard.

"She was murdered? What are you talking about? When?"

"Deputy Skeeter should not have said that, but now that it's out, can you please tell me the precise moment you last saw her?"

"She can't be murdered. Like dead? Are you sure? Maybe she's just missing." Bennett starts to try to suggest all the other plausible options.

"We have a preliminary identification. Her picture matches the girl that we found earlier today," I say, choosing my words very carefully and speaking slowly to try to get her to understand. "Bennett, I have to ask you."

"I saw her earlier this morning," she says, unable to meet my eyes any longer. She stares at her hands and then down at her feet. I can tell that I'm about to lose her.

"Bennett, you cannot share this with anyone here. Not yet."

"But somebody-- who did it? Was it someone from here?"

"We do not know any details and my partner should not have shared this information with you. I'm going to ask you to go with Dr. Abbott and stay with him for the time being, because we really do need to keep this information quiet until we're able to put together a better investigation."

I expect her to protest, but she doesn't. Instead, she just follows me and Dr. Abbott who slings his arm around her shoulder and practically supports her, carrying her back to the cabin.

"What were you thinking?" I snap at Gavin as soon as we get back to the main road, going through the camp away from anyone who could possibly hear us.

"I just wanted her to know that this was serious."

"Now what? Now she's going to tell everyone about what happened. How is she going to keep this a secret? She's a seventeen-year-old girl and her roommate was killed. You had no right to tell her that. We're waiting for her parents to show up and to confirm the identification."

"Well, what if she was involved?"

"Listen, I'm here to help you. Okay? I'm here to guide you about how to do this, but I don't want you messing all of this up for me. I'm not going to take you to any more interviews if you don't follow my lead."

"What are you going to tell them when they ask point-blank?"

"I'm going to tell them that she's missing for the time being and we're performing an investigation. No clear details. Okay? For all they know, she could have gone on a walk."

"You want to see their reaction when you call them on it?"

"Yes. When I call them, *a specific person*, on it. Right now, we have no idea the relationship between all these people. Was Bennett her friend? Were her roommates her friends? Did they turn on her? Was it a boyfriend? I don't know anything. When you tell her friends something as big as this, they start to shut down, especially if they're real friends and they had nothing to do with this.

"If she was her real friend and she was not involved in this murder, it's going to take her a few good hours to even process the information, hours that we don't have. I need to know who her friends were, who her enemies were, what guys she was interested in. Was she even interested in guys? Everyone is a suspect, but we need to create a web of relationships first, and these kids in this camp are the only ones who can help us. Dr. Abbott doesn't know. I mean, he knows that she's a good camp counselor. The kids like her, but it's her friends and the enemies here who are going to tell us the real details. We can't sequester every single one of them apart from everyone else."

"You really think that someone at the camp did this?"

I take a deep breath, telling myself to not smack him because he's just ignorant.

"I have no idea. I know as much as you do. We have to rule everyone out. If no one here seems suspicious, if no one knows anything, then maybe, maybe it was an outsider, but that makes the case a lot harder. Ten times harder, especially if it's someone that no one else knew."

"How are we going to find him? How are we going to track him?"

"We have to take the evidence where it goes. For that, we need all of these kids to tell us what they know without being shocked by what might have happened to her. Okay? So keep your mouth shut for the time being so we can get to the bottom of this."

9

CHARLOTTE

I'm still angry with Gavin. Furious is more like it. But that doesn't change the fact that I have to proceed with interviewing Antonia Vaughan next.

Dr. Abbott introduces her as Tony.

We find her by the basketball court refereeing two groups of ten year olds who couldn't score a basket if their life depended on it. Nevertheless, they're clearly having fun and Tony appears to be patient and a good coach from afar. She's surprised to see Dr. Abbott and to meet me. I'm thankful for the fact that whatever Bennett knows has not reached her yet.

Gavin, who's been walking around with his head hanging low this whole time, suddenly perks up and starts to play the exuberant nice guy.

"Hi, I'm Deputy Skeeter," he says with a big smile on his face, "and this is Detective Pierce. We just have a few questions for you about your roommate, Sarah Dunn."

I flash him a look and he lowers his pep level a little bit to make it appropriate to what we're about to tell her.

"When was the last time that you saw her?" I ask.

Tony shifts her weight from one foot to the other. She is much bigger than Bennett and the same standard issue camp shirt is tight around her midsection and her wide hips. Her hair is curly and frizzy. Even though there is barely any humidity in the mountains, it's still managing to frizz out in all directions.

Tony confirms the story that Bennett told me. The last time she saw her was early this morning, before breakfast.

"I'm collecting signatures to try to get more financial aid for low-income students and campers of color to come participate in the camp. This place is quite expensive and we're grateful for it. I mean, it's great, but I want it to be more inclusive and open to people from a variety of backgrounds."

"That's what you were doing?"

She nods.

"I actually have my clipboard right over here."

She walks over to the bench and her bag and pulls it out, showing me 200 signatures from the campers.

"I mean, all of these kids are in support of this. I'm going to show this to Dr. Abbott and the rest of the administration with a presentation later. Hopefully, we can make some changes, some positive changes in the spring, for next year."

"Wow, that's very admirable," I say.

The coach who steps in to fill in for her runs up to us as a runaway ball almost hits me in the head. Luckily, Gavin catches it in time and tosses it to the other counselor.

"Sorry about that!" the counselor yells.

"Yes, no worries," I say, looking back at the list of signatures. On the first page are the three signatures of her bunkmates.

"Sarah signed this one, right?"

"Yes." She nods.

"She was one of the first ones. To be honest, I'm not sure Elizabeth cared about it that much, but she signed it since we're roommates, but Sarah was really on board. She cares about these issues just like I do."

"She's active with different causes?" I ask. "Is that what she likes to do in her spare time?"

"No, I wouldn't say that. I'm very socially engaged, and I just love all this stuff. I want to pursue a career in government, eventually. Sarah's much more easygoing."

"What do you think she wants to do?"

"I have no idea. Her parents really want her to go to USC. So far, the only thing she knows for sure is that that's exactly what she doesn't want to do." Tony laughs. "She told me that a number of times."

"No college at all?"

"It's not like she needs it. Her dad is quite wealthy. He can always set her up doing investments with him, or something like that."

"Well, you do need to have some knowledge about finance or math for that, right?"

"Yes, that's what I kept telling her. The thing is that Sarah has more on her mind than her career nowadays."

So far, she hasn't asked why we're here. Which is a little surprising, but I am talking to a teenager, and they tend to be very self-involved. I'm here to ask, so I can't read too much into it, but the fact that she continuously speaks of her in present tense means that she either has no idea what has happened or she is a very good actor.

"Sarah's been really depressed," Tony says. "Just worn out by everything. She was really happy to be here, but she was nervous, too."

"What do you mean?"

"You have to talk to her. I can't really tell you all the details. It wouldn't be nice."

"The thing is that I can't talk to her," I say.

"What do you mean?"

"Well, she's missing."

Gavin and I exchange looks. He is cowering a little bit in the background probably feeling the pain of my wrath from our earlier conversation.

"What do you mean she's missing?" Tony asks.

She unfolds her arms and lets them fall to her sides. The acne on her face has been covered up with a thick layer of foundation, but the bumps are still visible. I struggled with that myself and wouldn't go back to being this age for all the money in the world.

I can't go into the details. I debate with myself how much to tell her. The fact that Bennett already knows the truth means that it's more likely to spread everywhere. I need her to tell me more information about Sarah and the details surrounding her disappearance as opposed to breaking down and dealing with the trauma of her murder.

"Let me just say that we're looking for her, and that's why we're talking to her roommates, anyone who might have had contact with her. Can you tell me anything else? You said that she was depressed. Do you think she might have been suicidal?"

"Suicidal? No, I don't think so. I mean, she would joke about it sometimes but she just had a dark sense of humor. She just cried a lot. I thought she was homesick, but she said she was excited to be here. She just had a lot of swinging emotions back and forth."

"Okay." I nod. "Did that have to do with her parents? With the people here?"

"Yes, her parents had a big thing about it. The divorce was over a long time ago, but there was still this constant back and forth with the lawyers about time with her, about alimony. She got to the point where she didn't want to go to her dad's house anymore because he had all these girlfriends. Her dad got mad and said that her mom was alienating her affection. She was stopping her from going. She was just this pawn in their tug of war. It was around that time that she-- I don't think I should tell you this."

She hesitates and then looks down at the ground. She's wearing thick sneakers. When she digs them into the ground and scoops up some dirt on them, their bright white color becomes covered in a layer of dust.

"Please tell me anything that you think is relevant, even if you don't think it's relevant. We are putting together this puzzle, this mosaic of who she is. We need more information."

"She cut herself, okay?" Tony says with exasperation. "I caught her. She had a little razor blade. She cut herself on her arms and legs. She said that she did it to make herself feel better. Every time she let out a little blood the anxiety and the tension would go away. I told her that she needed to talk to someone. She needed to get treatment. That this isn't a good way to go. But she said that she'd just get them lasered off, all the scar tissue that formed and that no one would ever know."

"Is that even possible?" I ask.

"I have no idea. I don't go to private school. I don't have a dermatologist and a plastic surgeon like all these other kids here. Maybe it's possible," Tony says. "She seemed to think so, and she had a lot of these little scars."

"Did she cover herself up in any way?" I ask.

"What do you mean?"

"Did she wear pants, long sleeves?"

"No, she couldn't do that." Tony shakes her head. "This is camp. We have standard-issue T-shirts and shorts. It's too hot for anything like that. She just pulled her shorts down a little lower than other girls and she always got an oversized T-shirt even before they were popular. She never wore any crop tops, nothing like that when we didn't have to be in uniform. I saw the way she would stand, often crossing her arms and just putting her legs one in front of the other. I realized that she stood like that and sat that way in order to make the scars a little bit less noticeable. Unless you really looked, you wouldn't see them and if you did, you'd think maybe they were some sort of scabs or something like that. They weren't horrible."

"Okay, I understand."

I talk to Tony a little bit longer but nothing else comes to the surface. This explains the T-shirt and the shorts and how uncovered her legs were. Of course, if she had just started doing it the tissue wasn't so bad and there weren't so many marks across her body that it was actually possible to still wear normal clothes and not have anyone pay attention. At the end of the conversation, I decide against telling Tony about her death. She heads back in to finish her duties as a counselor for the afternoon session. When I ask Dr. Abbott about Bennett, he says that he's going to keep her in his office for the rest of the day until we say it's okay. I thank him for his cooperation.

"We got a lot of good information here."

I turn to Gavin on our way over to talk to the last roommate, Elizabeth.

"So far, we haven't hit on any drama. Besides her roommates, who were her friends? Who were her enemies? Neither Tony nor Bennett seemed to know but someone must. What about a love interest? There must be. They're at the age where you have one love interest after another, or you love one person with an obsession that's almost toxic."

"Which camp did Sarah fall into?"

"I'm not sure but we are going to find out."

10

CHARLOTTE

We head over to the craft area where Dr. Abbott told us we'd find Elizabeth Mosely, but when we get there, a round-faced, wide-eyed girl tells us that she's filling in for her because she wasn't feeling well and we can find her back in her room. Walking across the camp I stop by a large bulletin board with notes attached to it under a Plexiglass screen.

There are signs for extracurricular clubs that are available to participate in while at camp: a sign-up sheet for the newspaper, a call back sheet for the musical that's going to be put on in two weeks, as well as a call for artwork for work to be displayed at the art show, which could be paintings, sculptures, dioramas, and everything in between.

"Nice camp, huh?" Gavin says. "You ever been to anything like this?"

I shake my head. "No. You?"

"No. My dad was a cop. I went to the local YMCA."

"Did you like it?" I ask.

He nods. "Yes. Made some friends. Mostly hung out with the kids I played with at school."

"Nothing like this." I shrug.

I know where he's coming from. A tinge of jealousy runs through me as well.

"What would it be like to go to a place like this, the memories you make, the friendships you build? Not to be macabre, but you could also get murdered in a place like this," I add and give him a wink. He smiles. Dark humor is all we have sometimes, and we have to rely upon it. Even if it's a little inappropriate, it's just talk between us cops, of course.

I knock on the cabin door and I hear a faint voice on the other side say, "Come in."

I crack the door and Elizabeth smiles and waves at us from the upper bunk. She doesn't bother lifting her head, but does turn, at least, toward us. We go through the introductions and this piques her interest. She sits up, swinging her long legs over the side and letting them dangle over the bottom bunk. The walls next to the beds are plastered with photos and magazine cut-outs. A vision board, as well as letters and postcards from friends back home, I assume.

"Where could Sarah have gone?" Elizabeth asks, brushing her manicured fingernails through her long blonde hair.

It's perfectly straight and just thick enough to look like she could be a hair model for a shampoo commercial. Her skin is tan, her face glossy, but not at all shiny. She looks like she is an Instagram model for the no makeup look. Elizabeth is beautiful, and she undoubtedly knows it. We go through the questions once again asking about the last time that she saw Sarah and everything else that we asked the other roommates. The stories match. She doesn't look at all concerned but tells me that she saw her earlier this morning.

"She seemed fine." Elizabeth adds. "Her normal self, a little down, but I was hoping that things with Dominic could have gone a little bit better."

I raise an eyebrow. This is the first time I've heard that name or anyone mention a boy whatsoever.

"Can you tell me more about Dominic?"

"Sure."

"What is his last name?"

"It's Dominic Marcel. He's one of the counselors. Sarah's had a crush on him for ages, but there's a rumor that he has a girlfriend and things didn't go so well."

"Oh, okay. Did Sarah know about the girlfriend?"

"I'm not sure. We're roommates and all, but I don't like to gossip. When people tell me something in private, I want to keep it that way, so they trust me for the next bit of information."

"Uh-huh." I nod. "Dominic had a girlfriend?"

"Yes, until a couple of days ago. She broke up with him. Misty is a counselor at the camp, too, and she had this whole thing about not telling anyone. He was quite distressed. I heard it from his roommate, who I was sort of hooking up with. No one was supposed to know. Once you see him, you'll know that Dominic is not someone that you would be embarrassed to call your boyfriend."

She jumps off the top bunk and then heads over to the desk in the corner and takes a swig from the metal water bottle.

"Anyway, Misty has this whole problem. They were together the whole year while they were apart, but for some reason she broke up with him now? He had all these suspicions about the fact that she was cheating on him or something like that."

"What about Sarah? Did she know about any of this?"

"If she did, she didn't know it from me. I feel bad for the girl, honestly, but I just couldn't tell her. She's not the one to keep a secret. Yesterday she came home early in the morning, before breakfast, and she was on cloud nine. I asked what it was about and she said that Dominic and she had hugged. She met him out by the dock and they had this moment. She didn't mention anything about Misty at the time, so I have no idea what he told her or what he didn't."

"You didn't want to warn her that this guy that she was into might have a girlfriend?"

"Yes, I thought about it, girl code and everything, but his roommate told me all this stuff in confidence. Okay, I like him. Dean is sweet, and hot, and available, and he likes me, so I didn't want to ruin it. I figured she doesn't have to know all the details. Besides, maybe if she didn't think that he had a girlfriend, she would actually make a move on him, which is something that she's been dreaming of for as long as I can remember."

"She has been into Dominic for a while?"

"Yes, like three years, at least that I know of. I think she tried to date guys in high school, but she just keeps thinking about him. We've been going to camp together since we were kids, and then we became counselors together, and it's just been a whole complicated mess."

"Does he know that she likes him?"

"I don't know. He's really dense. Everyone else does and someone might have told him, but I don't think he actually knows."

"What about what happened yesterday?"

"Today is her birthday, so we're going to have a whole cake and celebration for her later this afternoon, but yesterday she took off early, went on one of her walks to think about life. She almost didn't make it back to breakfast. When she did, she was so excited. She said she couldn't go into everything, but they'd hugged. I asked if they kissed and she said she's happy with just a hug, which for me, I wouldn't be happy, but I can see how it's a huge move in that relationship because nothing has happened in three years between them."

Elizabeth talks with her hands. She gesticulates and talks with a bit of a Southern California accent or perhaps it's just the accent of a confident, self-realized young woman who knows her worth. Some people might call her arrogant, but in this moment I don't see that. What I also realize is that she has no idea about what happened to her friend. She mentioned the birthday party, the cake, and the get-together. I asked more about that to prepare myself for how much of this I have to break to the kids at the camp.

"What kind of party are you having? Is it just the four of you?"

"No, it's everyone. Whenever it's anyone's birthday at the camp, everyone is invited and mostly everyone goes. We have a big bonfire, cake, s'mores, and some games. It's really fun. And since we're counselors, we get to indulge a little bit longer than the little kids who have to go to bed, but almost everyone at the camp goes. Summer birthdays are crap since you don't have your school friends, and so this is just a way to make up for it."

"Okay." I nod, exchanging glances with Gavin, who looks similarly shell-shocked.

"Everyone is expecting a party?"

"Yes, of course. Why? I never asked you, but did something happen to Sarah? Is she okay?"

That's when it hits her that I haven't told her much about her at all and she came out and shared almost everything she knows.

"The thing is that," I shift my weight from one foot to the other, suddenly feeling a drip of sweat down my back and my underarms, "Sarah is missing."

"Missing?"

"She hasn't shown up to her posts and Dr. Abbott and some of the other higher-ups here couldn't find her, so they called us. I want you to keep this information private for now, okay? I need to talk to Dominic and Misty and whoever else to try to piece the story together about where she might be."

"Have you checked the lake?"

11

CHARLOTTE

U p until this point, I had no suspicions about Elizabeth. She seemed so frank, an open book. No hesitations, no secret information but then, in a moment, everything changed. She mentioned the lake as a place where I should look for Sarah. The same place where we'd found her.

"What do you mean the lake?" I ask, closing my journal for a moment with the pen inside. I didn't pull out my phone to record, as sometimes interviewing suspects or potential suspects makes it more difficult when there's a recording device present; it puts them on edge. I figured that it would spook the teenagers here. Elizabeth hesitates, her eyes dart from one side of the room to the other, avoiding both mine and Gavin's.

"Elizabeth, can you please tell me anything that you know, however minor the detail? It's just very important for us to get to the truth." She exhales quickly, and it sounds a bit like a snort.

"Elizabeth, what did you mean by 'have we checked the lake'?"

"She just wasn't comfortable being out on the lake. I don't want to be macabre about it, but she loved going to the lake and being on the shore and she could swim well enough. She was a lifeguard even, but she just had a bad feeling about the lake. She said that people drowned in it, and she didn't want to take kids out canoeing. She preferred to do other things."

"But she was a good swimmer?" Gavin asks.

"Yes, she had a lifeguard certification. Everyone here has to be able to do CPR and pull someone out of the water. This is a camp, so it has to be safe. She was okay at swimming in the pool and she enjoyed going to the lake, but she said there was something dark that drew her there."

Gavin and I exchange looks again.

"Can you tell me what Sarah was like personality-wise? Any quirks?"

"She was a total Debbie Downer," Elizabeth says. "Everything was just bad. Everything was a concern. She's not as annoying as Tony, for instance, with all of her goody two shoes raising money for this, raising awareness for that, but she had a really dark streak. Let's just put it that way."

"What does that mean?" I ask.

"She joked a lot about suicide. I don't want to gossip, but she did. She joked around about it a lot, and Tony was going to report her to Dr. Abbott if she didn't stop, and she even told her that. She stopped, but I don't know if she stopped having those thoughts. It's hard because it was always a joke."

My heart sinks. With a history of cutting herself and now thinking about suicide, I start to wonder what the medical examiner's report is actually going to find. The bruises and the stuff around her neck, could those wounds be self-inflicted? Maybe, but she was found by the lake. The marks on her neck may have made sense if she hung herself, but how could she do that and then throw herself head up in the lake and supposedly drown?

"Do you really think that she was capable of suicide?" I ask.

Elizabeth shrugs. "Maybe. She was capable of a lot of things. She could do anything, but her parents really messed her up. They were so toxic. I wouldn't say any of our parents are well adjusted, but most of us at this point have just learned to accept them for the idiots that they are and move on with life. You can't change them, just put up with them as much as you can and do what you want, but she was really affected by what they were doing. Just concerned, worried, and that made me worry."

I let her go for now and tell her to relax, but I might be in touch later. She says that she'll be here, and Gavin and I walk out.

"What do you think?" I ask, facing him.

"I don't know how that could have been suicide, to be honest," Gavin admits. "It didn't look like a suicide at all."

"Have you seen any suicide cases before?"

"Yes. Some person ran in front of a bus, got smashed out pretty bad, but there were witnesses, the bus driver, the shopkeepers. He just jumped out, and that wasn't his first suicide attempt either."

"The cutting concerns me," I say. "A lot of people who cut themselves do commit suicide."

"Yes, I agree, but what about how we found the body?" Gavin adds. "She was just lying there like that.

How could she have done it? Then if she had died, how did she transport herself to the lake?"

"That's got me stumped as well."

"There's another possibility," Gavin points out.

I know exactly what he's thinking.

"Maybe Elizabeth wants us to believe it's suicide because she knows a lot more than she's letting on."

"Yes, that's definitely an option."

We walk back to Dr. Abbott's office and grab some lunch out of the vending machine. Bennett is still being held in one of the rooms, and I hear her complaining to Dr. Abbott about wanting to watch something on her phone. Apparently, he had confiscated it in order to prevent her from talking. I overhear the back and forth with Dr. Abbott finally giving in, but only after numerous promises from her and assurances that she would not tell anyone about this.

"He lays on that guilt trip real thick, doesn't he?"

Gavin smiles biting into his cheese and ham sandwich. I opt for a Snickers bar and an apple instead, hoping that the nutritional value of the apple would somehow balance out the junk in the Snickers bar. In the distance, Dr. Abbott hovers over

Bennett and she continues to promise him that she won't say anything until the parents are notified.

SPEAK of the devil and he shall appear. In this case, she.

Mrs. Dunn arrives in a head-to-toe white suit, stiletto heels, and a Birkin bag to match. Her hair is blown out, and under the plastic face and makeup, I can see a clear sign of concern.

We had notified her that her daughter was missing but didn't go far enough to tell her what we had found. I take one more bite of my Snickers bar, swallowing it almost whole, wipe my hands on my pants because a napkin is nowhere to be found, and then introduce myself to Mrs. Dunn.

12

***

CHARLOTTE

I pull her into Dr. Abbott's office where we can have some privacy and I break the bad news. The shock overwhelms her before any sadness hits. She stares at me with her big doe-eyed look, her cosmetically de-aged face almost expressionless at first. I know that a lot of people get plastic surgery procedures, Botox, fillers, and everything else, and I'm not judgmental of any of that at all. In fact, I've been thinking about some Botox myself given the long lines that suddenly showed up across my forehead without my consent or desire, but Mrs. Dunn has overdone it.

She still kept getting procedures until she looks like every other rich woman from LA. When it comes to expressing sadness, her face basically contorts in on itself with her lips moving up and down as she buries her face in her hands.

"I'm so sorry."

I'm suddenly feeling bad for judging her looks once again. Despite her wealth and status, she's just another victim's mother who wants answers for what happened to her beautiful daughter who was taken too soon.

"What do you mean she was found dead?" Mrs. Dunn manages to ask.

"She was found this morning. A photographer found her. She was on the edge of the lake lying on her back. I have some pictures for you to confirm the identification, but we are pretty certain. That's why I asked you to come up here."

I pull out my phone and show her the pictures and she begins to cry. She'll still have to go to the medical examiner's office where her daughter is currently being held and identify the body in person, or perhaps on camera, which has recently become the way to do it in order to preserve evidence and make it easier for the person performing the autopsy. But for now, judging from her reaction, I know that it's her daughter.

It takes Mrs. Dunn a while to get a hold of herself to a point where she's able to speak again. As she cries,

I excuse myself in order to bring her some coffee and food and give her some space to grieve.

"This is the worst part of the job, isn't it?" Gavin says. "I don't know how you can do it day in, day out."

"Well, luckily, murders aren't very common in Mesquite County," I say. "But yes, this never gets easier. You just tune out the pain and create some distance and separation."

It's one of the reasons why I stepped out for some coffee and some baked goods, to give her some time to process it and pull myself away from it all and take a deep breath. Unfortunately, in this case, the baked goods are from the vending machine, cold and hard as a rock, but it's the thought that counts, I hope. I take a deep breath and head back in.

Mrs. Dunn has pulled herself together a bit. She stares at me blankly when I come back with the coffee and cookies. I offer my condolences once again and then sit across from her at the table and ask if there's anything that she knows that might help me figure out what happened or who might have done this to her daughter. She shakes her head and looks out the window. Campers are laughing and running after one another. One girl grabs another's hand. He gives her a warm embrace and though their giggles can't be heard inside the room, I can see the twinge of pain they bring to Mrs. Dunn's face.

"She loved this place," Mrs. Dunn says. "She was obsessed with it. I sent her here only because my husband and I were having trouble with all of his affairs, and we needed some space. We didn't want to be fighting in front of her all summer. She was in seventh grade and I thought she would hate it, honestly. But she made these friends and she said it was the best thing ever. She had friends at school, but it wasn't the same. She kept talking about wanting to go to boarding school. She had no idea what she was talking about. She had no idea what that meant."

"What do you mean?" I ask.

"My parents sent me away to boarding school. They sent me away because they didn't want to deal with me during the year. It was terrible and cruel, and I would never want that for her and that's why I didn't want her to go to this stupid camp."

"Well, maybe not all camps and boarding schools are the same, and neither are people." I suggest.

She flashes her eyes at me and glares. I feel like we're starting to get off on a bad track and so I pivot the conversation.

"So, she's been going here for years?"

"Yes, she has. This is her third year as a counselor and her first year as a senior counselor."

"What does that mean exactly?"

"Just more responsibilities, I guess. More free time. She and her friends basically rule this place as far as I know."

"Have you ever met her roommates?"

She shakes her head, picking at the table with her long, polished oval-shaped nail. They're a couple of inches over her fingers and manicured to perfection. She takes a sip of her coffee but doesn't touch the cookie.

"So, she was looking forward to coming to camp this year?" I ask.

"She was counting down the days. She was acting like being home was the worst thing ever. It wasn't, you know."

"Was she planning on going to college?" I ask, knowing from her friends that this was a point of contention with her parents.

"Her father and I were insisting on USC. It's a good school and people from good stock go there."

I haven't heard that phrasing in a long time, referring to people as stock.

"I got the impression that she wasn't interested."

"Yes, that's what she told her friends. I have no doubt about that, but this is probably the one thing that her father and I agreed on. She absolutely had to go."

"To college or to USC?"

"Both. She wasn't happy about it, but we didn't ask her for much and gave her everything."

I want to ask 'Why were you so set on USC?' but I already know the answer. They're both graduates and she probably thinks that it is a good place to meet a guy. A future husband.

"Do you know if she had a romantic relationship with anyone at school?"

"No. I don't. She didn't talk to me about things like that. She was embarrassed. I did read in her diary that she's never kissed anyone before and that was, of course, shocking."

"What do you mean by that?" I ask.

What I find shocking is the fact that she would so willingly admit that she had read her teenage daughter's diary, but I let that go for now.

"Well, at her age, I had a lot of boyfriends. Guys were interested. I was interested in some of them. Just dating around how teenagers do. I see my friends' kids. They do the same thing. Technology is different, clothes are different, cars are different, but kids are the same. Sarah wasn't like that, though. For a while, I thought maybe she was into girls, but no. She wrote in her diary how much she liked this one kid named Dominic and he was at camp here."

"Do you know if anything happened with him?"

"No. Ever since she came here, she hasn't updated her diary one bit."

"Is this online?"

"Yes. It's in her Apple notes on her phone under the same password she uses for everything else."

"You never had any qualms about checking her private journal?"

"I'm a mother, Detective Pierce. It's my job to know what my daughter is up to."

I nod in agreement even though I don't agree at all, but then again, I don't have a child let alone a teenager to think about. Even though Mrs. Dunn is well aware of the fact that her daughter is now gone, it doesn't stop her from talking about her in that slightly demeaning sort of way that I find off-putting.

Mrs. Dunn opens her bag, pulls out a bottle of prescription medication, and pops a few in her mouth.

"Don't worry. A doctor said it was okay."

I nod in agreement but then realize that she didn't know why she was coming up here in the first place. Yet here she is prepared for whatever bad news I was going to give her with medication that would solve all of her problems.

We talk a little bit more about Sarah, but every time I try to get any information about what she's like, what she likes to do, Mrs. Dunn continuously brings that information back to herself. Herself as a mother, wife, her ex-husband, who's clearly still on her mind because she talks about fighting with him as late as last week.

"Who do you think could have done this to her?" she asks.

When the medication, probably Valium, starts to kick in, she gets more relaxed, at ease, not so tense but not exactly at peace either, more absent-minded than anything else.

"I'm not sure; that's what we're here to find out."

"I just don't understand. Am I expected to believe that there's a killer somewhere at this camp killing counselors, or is this a stranger, a hobo passing through this little town, or worse yet, a local?" she suggests. "Somebody who knows about this camp and the campers and has been watching them for some time."

"Mrs. Dunn, I don't know if it's any of those people."

I want to say that she has clearly been watching way too much television, but I don't want to be insulting.

"Those are definitely legitimate concerns," I say as calmly as possible, knowing that maintaining a cold demeanor generally puts people I speak to at ease, as well as gives them confidence in my ability to solve this problem. "We're going to be talking to everyone. There were clues left at the scene and we're going to get to the bottom of it."

"So, you're going to find out who did this?" she asks.

I have learned long ago not to make promises about that because there were a number of cases that I worked on with the LAPD that went cold and were never solved. It's nothing that I'm proud of but there are only so many things I can do if the evidence isn't there.

"I can't exactly promise you that," I say. "What I can say is that I will do everything in my power to get to the bottom of what has happened."

I send Gavin with Mrs. Dunn to the coroner at the local hospital where Sarah's body is being held.

We need a positive ID from a family member that isn't just through a picture. In the meantime, I have to talk to Dominic Marcel.

13

CHARLOTTE

I find Dominic near the lake. It's late in the afternoon now, almost dinner time. He's alone in the boathouse doing some maintenance, washing off one of the kayaks with fresh water from the hose. He's wearing Ray-Bans over his eyes and his baseball cap over his long shaggy hair. He's slim but fit, has a Puka shell necklace around his neck, and definitely gives me Harry Styles' vibes from back in the day. I can see why he's become such a local heartthrob.

When I introduce myself, he's surprised to meet me, and I can tell the fact that the cops are here investigating a missing persons case has not reached him yet. Either Tony and Elizabeth have kept their mouth shut or the secrets are safe with whomever they told, at least for the time being. Once we have a

firm identification from Sarah's mother, I know that
we have to make a formal statement to people at
camp through Dr. Abbott. The birthday party is
coming up and everyone is going to be wondering
where the belle of the ball is.

"Can I talk to you for a second, Dominic?" I ask.

He leans back putting a lot of his weight on an oar,
propping his sunglasses to the top of his baseball
cap. It's worn and shredded in that cool guy way. I'm
suddenly reminded of the guy that I had a crush on,
who looked very similar to him back when I was
seventeen.

"I'm here to talk to you about Sarah Dunn."

He nods but shows no emotion one way or another.

"I've been called here to investigate what might have
happened to her."

"What do you mean?" Dominic asks.

"Well, as of this morning, she's missing. She didn't
attend any of her work assignments. Substitutes had
to fill in and Dr. Abbott got concerned when it
turned out that no one had seen her."

Dominic shifts his weight from one foot to the other.
He's wearing loose-fitting shorts, and he buries his
hands deep inside of them slouching just a little bit.

"When was the last time that you saw her?"

"Can't say that I saw her today at all." He shrugs and I'm starting to feel like he's becoming a little evasive.

"When was the last time you spent any time with her?" I ask.

"Yesterday morning."

"At the dock?"

"I was out there after a night of staying up, just thinking and she showed up. Surprised me, actually. We haven't hung out like that. It was nice talking to her. She gave me some advice."

"About what?"

"It's private."

"I know, Dominic, but I need to know as many details as possible. It'll really help me find her."

"I don't see how that's related. I'm just a counselor here, like anyone else, and I haven't even seen her for a day."

"You didn't see her this morning at all, breakfast, at the dock, anywhere else?"

"No." He shakes his head.

"You did have a nice conversation with her before?"

"Yes."

He's shutting down. I can feel it. Slouching more, narrowing his eyes, answering my questions with one-word answers. I need to turn this around. I need to get him to trust me.

"I was made aware of the fact that Sarah had a crush on you. Liked you a lot. Did you know that?"

He shrugs. "Maybe, maybe not."

"Dominic, I really need your help here. You want to help me find her, don't you?"

"Yes, of course, but the way you're coming at me, it's like you think I did something."

"Not at all," I say. "I already interviewed her roommates, all three of them, and Dr. Abbott. I'm just trying to talk to as many campers and counselors as possible in order to try to piece together what might have happened."

He shrugs, looks up at me, and narrows his eyes, but this time something is different. It's like he's analyzing if he can trust me or not. I broaden my shoulders, open myself up, and let my hands fall loosely at my sides. I'm not hiding anything. I'm not trying to trick him. I want him to see that I'm here out of an earnest effort to find his friend.

"Yes, I knew that she liked me. She was nervous about it. I didn't know it until we met at the dock, but when we talked and I told her about my ex-girlfriend and all the drama that we were going through, I got the sense that maybe she was interested."

"Okay. Thank you. I really appreciate that. Anything else of significance happen?"

"We hung out and chatted. She made me see that I was being an ass to Misty but, of course, that didn't change anything."

"You got the sense that she was interested, but she was also helping you resolve your problem with your girlfriend?" I ask for clarification.

He nods.

"Sarah was good like that. She was sweet, kind, and--"

His voice drops off.

"Did something happen between you two? How did you leave things?"

"Fine. We're friends, coworkers. We share this whole experience. There's not many of us who have been here so long. It brings you closer."

"I'm getting that sense here. I agree. Did she try to kiss you?"

"No."

"Did you try to kiss her?"

"No," he says.

I try to read his body language, but it's cryptic, full of conflicting information. His arms are crossed. He's hunched over one moment and then the next he's standing with his legs wide open, arms at his sides looking at me with those innocent eyes.

"I heard that you might have made a connection."

"You heard that from who?"

He takes a step back. Shocked.

"It doesn't matter from who, but she seemed to get the signal that you might have been interested as well."

"Did she tell one of her roommates that we made out or something? We didn't. I just gave her a hug."

"Okay. Maybe she elaborated, tried to make more of it than it was, and it wasn't anything more."

"No, not at all." He shrugs. "Do you mind? I have to get back to work here, otherwise, I'm going to be late for dinner."

I see that I'm losing control here. He's shutting down. This is going to be the end of our conversation unless I say something else.

"What if I told you that we found Sarah Dunn's body this morning in the lake? That she had been murdered. That she was dead."

"What?" Dominic looks up from the oars, still holding one that he was arranging into the rack. "You're joking, right?"

"No."

"You said that she was missing."

"She was missing originally, but yes, we found her body."

"I had nothing to do with that," he snaps.

"I'm not saying that you did. I'm just saying that it's very important for me to know everything that happened with Sarah. Every detail, no matter how small or how private because I'm trying to piece together her last days on earth in order to figure out what happened."

I try to gauge his reaction but he's difficult to read. He looks surprised. His eyes grow big, mouth drops open, but something still feels off. Am I telling him something that he already knows or is he just a shocked teenager who maybe wasn't entirely honest with me about everything but had nothing to do with her death?

"It's very important that you tell me everything, Dominic. Your friend is gone and I'm here to uncover what happened to her. I need to piece together where she was, what she did, who she interacted with."

"I had nothing to do with this," he snaps.

"I'm not saying that you did, but did you see her yesterday, last night, or at all this morning?"

He hesitates.

"I'm only interested in what happened to Sarah. I'm not here to arrest you for anything illegal you might have done. If you were doing drugs, anything like that, I'm a homicide detective. I don't care about anything else."

This seems to put him at ease. You never know what people are afraid of and what lies are just covers for something else. People will try to cover their tracks over something that you as a detective may not care about. They lie but for the wrong reason. Teenagers are particularly susceptible to this line of thinking.

"What happens if I tell you that Sarah and I were together at another time?" he asks.

"When?"

"No, tell me what happens?"

"Nothing happens." I shrug. "I'm going to try to corroborate your story. I'm going to try to find out and connect the dots about what she did in the days before her disappearance and her death. That's all, Dominic."

We're going in circles getting nowhere fast but that's how it is with some people; they need to trust you, they need to build faith. They're not just going to come out and tell you everything you want because certain things have to be kept a secret. I don't let him off the hook. I can see that he's trying to leave the boathouse but I follow him and press him.

I'm getting close. He's about to say something. It only then dawns on me that he's not eighteen years old yet and I'm questioning him as a possible murder suspect. A part of me hopes that he doesn't come out and admit to killing her, right here right now because I'm not sure any of that would stand up in court since he doesn't have his parent or guardian with him.

"Sarah and I hung out again. Not just in the morning yesterday but later in the afternoon."

"Okay." I nod. "That's good to hear."

"We snuck out. We were assigned to canoeing together. I called in earlier saying that I wasn't feeling good, and she said that she needed a break and she hadn't had a substitute for a while so they had someone fill in for us. We were supposed to go back to our cabins, but we went to town instead."

"To Quail Lake?"

"Yes. We rode our bikes."

"And what did you do?"

"Just hung out, got some ice cream, went to a thrift store, just got out of camp and all the responsibilities and everything else that goes with it."

"And why didn't you tell me this earlier?"

"I just didn't want to be involved. I mean, nothing happened. Just spent time together but I didn't want Misty to know."

"Misty's your girlfriend?"

He nods and corrects me, "Ex-girlfriend."

"The way Sarah looked at me, she was like a puppy dog in love. I liked that. Misty used to look at me like that, but she hasn't for a while. It was stupid but it just felt good to hang out with someone like that, you know, to be wanted, to be liked, adored. I was surprised but I enjoy spending time with her as well. She was pretty smart, had a dark sense of humor, made a lot of jokes about death and that kind of thing."

"What do you mean?" I ask.

Here's the dark sense of humor again, I think to myself. Something that her roommates have also confirmed.

"I don't know. She made jokes about suicide. It felt weird but I laughed along. I never met a girl who joked about killing herself before."

I clench my jaw. Suicidal ideation seems to be coming up a lot in the context of my victim and I need to talk to the medical examiner sooner rather than later to see if that's even a possibility. From the outside, it didn't look like it but who knows.

"Okay, but did you have a good time with her? What did you do in town exactly?"

"I told you. We just hung out, went to the coffee shop, went to the thrift store, killed some time, and got some pizza."

"That's a lot of places," I say.

He shrugs again.

"Did anything romantic happen?" I ask, point-blank. "I want you to tell me everything that happened and not hide anything. Did you have anything to drink? Any alcohol, smoke weed, cigarettes? It's all fine. I mean, you shouldn't be doing that, but you're not going to be in trouble for it. I just need to have a good idea of what happened."

He nods his head and looks down at the ground and then he's picking at his nails a little bit in a nervous way.

"When we got pizza, she went to the bathroom, then I followed her out back, and we were joking around. Then, we kissed. She was a good kisser. She had soft lips and I liked that. At first, I was worried about leading her on, but I figured she's a big girl. If she liked me and I like her, why not?"

"Do you think she had certain expectations?"

"No, I think she was happy to be kissed. At least she seemed that way. Afterward, we went back, finished our pizza, and then headed back to camp. That was it, I swear. No drugs, no alcohol, nothing like that."

"And you haven't seen her since?"

"Just at dinner with everyone else, but we didn't really talk."

"Do you think she expected something more from you?"

"Sometimes we worked the same posts, so I figured we would talk and maybe make plans again, but we didn't make many plans at that point."

"What about your ex-girlfriend? Did she know anything about this?"

"No, at least I didn't tell her. I don't think Sarah did either. It was just this moment we shared in a place where we shouldn't have been, where we would've been really in trouble had anyone found out. It was our secret."

I am uncertain as to whether I believe him. The thing about pulling out the truth, one little kernel at a time, is that you never know when you reach the end.

I pressed him and pushed him, and he told me more but what more has he kept to himself? Is there more? Maybe that was it, but why didn't he tell me this before? Why say that he only saw her on the dock that day and nothing else?

Dominic returns to Dr. Abbott's office with me at my request. I ask him to go and sit with Tony in the back room for now. They're the only ones who know the truth so far.

With the birthday dinner looming, we all have to figure out a way to tell the campers about what has happened to Sarah.

14

SARAH

Sarah was on cloud nine that morning ever since the unexpected hug that started out as an apology for something that was quite mean. She never thought she would be a girl who would put up with something like that, but suddenly she saw the power of a good apology, especially in all its sincerity. When Dominic hugged her and held her close, she listened to his heart, but it wasn't until he apologized and said how sorry he was that she forgave him.

Then he pulled away, looked straight into her eyes, and asked, "What are you doing later today?" The words were straight out of a movie. This had to be happening to someone else, the heroine in a romance novel, who was finally getting what she wanted. She had loved Dominic so long from afar and yet on some subconscious level, she never believed that she could really have him. This date, this get-together in the middle of the afternoon, was maybe not even romantic at all, but it was much more than she'd ever encountered up until this point, so she was going to savor this moment.

"Not doing anything special. I just have canoeing with you, if you remember."

This is the one activity they did three days a week together, and she used to obsess about her outfit and the way she wore her hair and makeup, despite the fact that they spent most of it covered in splashes from the lake.

Sarah analyzed every interaction and smile and witty comment from him, and now here he was asking her to actually do something with him.

"Just wondering if you want to play hooky and go to town."

"Really?" she asked.

He gave her a wink, that gorgeous, easygoing smile that he had flashed at so many girls, but rarely at her until this moment.

"Sure, I guess."

"I don't think we should take off at the same time," Dominic said. "They might get suspicious about that."

"Why don't you cancel before the class, and I'll get there and then make some excuse as to why I can't go ahead with it?"

"Will they be able to find a replacement in time?"

"Yes, there's always someone around, right?" He smiled and she couldn't believe her luck.

"What do you want to do in town?" she asked, trying to gauge whether he was just trying to spend time with her as a friend or perhaps more than that.

"Get some coffee, just talk, maybe grab some pizza if we get hungry. If you don't want to go, just let me know, I'm good either way."

That didn't make her feel good, but she wondered if he was just trying to put her at ease and take some of the pressure off, a real possibility.

Sarah had called off with a headache right after lunch, and this was the first time she'd ever taken a break this whole summer so she doubted anyone would find it at all suspicious. Unlike Elizabeth who pushed the legal limits of what is decent behavior as a camp counselor in terms of not having someone else do your job multiple times a day, she was conscientious and prompt.

She spent the time getting ready, trying to tame some of the frizz of her hair, cover up a few of the freckles, not all, with foundation, and popping her eyes with a little bit of eyeshadow and a lot of mascara. Her ideal look was to appear beautiful without really trying, and she wasn't entirely sure if she had succeeded at that even when she rode the back road out of camp on her bike.

There in the woods, right at the corner on the edge of the property, she spotted Dominic reclining back on his green bicycle, eating an apple, waiting for her.

"Hey, stranger," he said, and she nearly melted.

"I wasn't sure if you'd come." He tilted his head, his hair falling in his face.

"I'm here." Sarah smiled, and she knew that this afternoon would be one that she would not forget.

SARAH HAD no idea what to expect from what was about to happen, but she was excited for it. She hadn't been out on a date like this before and everything about Dominic made her feel on the edge of her seat.

The depression that seemed to follow her everywhere like a dark cloud had almost lifted and was quickly replaced by anxiety, the kind that made her palms sweaty and her heartbeat irregular.

Dominic, on the other hand, seemed full of an easy, assured confidence. Nothing bothered him, nothing stumped him. He had an answer for everything and so when she met him that afternoon, she let him lead the way. She followed him on his bike to town. They took trails over there. While he made jokes that she hardly understood, she laughed along, nevertheless.

The Angel View thrift store was the first stop. He made her try on funny hats and when she got brave enough, she wrapped a scarf around his neck. Trailing her hands around his chest was the kind of intimacy that she had never experienced before. It took her by surprise. It completely infatuated her and made her drunk on her own power. She watched the way that his eyes trailed her fingers and she realized that she wasn't the only one who had wanted him. He wanted her, too.

Is this the real life or is this just fantasy? Freddie Mercury sang in the background, almost narrating their trip through Angel View. Of course, she had to stop in the back where books upon books were piled on rickety shelves in no order whatsoever.

"I love how you can come here and you never know what you're going to find," she said, scanning the shelves and touching the spines but Dominic recoiled taking a step back.

"What's wrong? I thought you liked to read."

"I do, but old books are dusty, smelly, and the paper is usually yellow," he pointed out.

"Yes, I know. That's what makes them so great."

"No. Don't like it." He shook his head. "I mean, how can you even find anything on these shelves?"

"You can't, that's the whole point." Sarah laughed. "Otherwise, if we wanted something new, we'd go to Barnes & Noble or Amazon. The point of looking for books in thrift stores is that you don't know what you're going to get."

He laughed nervously, somewhat agreeing with her, but not really. She knew that but didn't care. She had spent so long trying to figure out how to get everybody at school and in camp aware of her, accepting of her, and for a second, it clicked that maybe it didn't matter after all. Maybe it was okay to have an opinion that differed from other people's and that was what made her unique and special. Just because people didn't agree with her, it didn't mean that one of them was right or one of them was wrong. Both opinions could exist and be valid at the same time.

When they walked out of the thrift store and Dominic asked Sarah about her parents, she shook her head. "No," she told him that she wasn't going to talk about them.

"Why not?"

"They occupy way too much of my mental space as it is and I just want to have a good time with you and that's it."

"Okay. Well, will you promise to tell me about them some other time?"

"Sure. Sometime I'm feeling masochistic."

That was the SAT vocab word of the day. She had a little calendar that she often forgot to rip off day to day and then it would have ten words to learn. She was a good thirty behind.

When they got to the coffee shop, they talked about more lighthearted things, school, friends, funny jokes, and memes from the internet. They hovered over their phones, their heads pressed close to one another. Being so close to Dominic made Sarah feel a little queasy and uncertain with her stomach full of butterflies. The good kind.

The pizza shop was her suggestion. Something to do to extend the afternoon, even though neither of them were particularly hungry. They grabbed a few slices, sat down on the same side of the booth, and it was at that point that Sarah no longer felt like she was here alone. Like he had wanted to be here as well. When she excused herself to go to the bathroom, she washed her hands, looked at herself in the mirror, and told herself to stay calm. It's working. Are they on a date? They had to be, right?

He liked her. He wasn't going to say that this is all just being friendly and nothing else. As soon as she exited the bathroom, holding the rickety wooden door behind her so it didn't make a loud slamming sound, she saw him standing in the poorly lit hallway. He smiled at her, gave her a wink, and she knew that he had been waiting. What she hadn't expected was for him to take another step closer and another and then pull her into his arms and kiss her on the lips. The way that she had imagined him doing for such a long time.

The kiss itself was what she expected, but not. His lips were firm and confident and yet gentle. Being in his arms made everything okay and yet exciting and over the top, at the same time. She pulled away from him only slightly to look into his eyes to make sure that she wasn't dreaming. Then she stood up on her tiptoes and kissed him again.

"You want to get out of here?" Dominic asked when they separated for a second time.

Feeling more at ease in his arms, she looked up at him, resting her head on his shoulder.

"And go where? Back to camp?"

"No." He shook his head. "Somewhere more private."

She licked her lower lip and looked up at him, her eyes twinkling. "The Wagon Wheel Motel is not too far away."

15

CHARLOTTE

After Dr. Abbott tells the campers that Sarah's birthday party and celebration are canceled, I head over to the pizza shop to get away from the inevitable questions and the drama that would inevitably have ensued. The details have not been covered yet. No murder was mentioned. Just a cancellation and an obscure statement about Sarah being gone.

I pull into the village located on the lake and park next to a toy store with old-style nutcrackers, matchbox cars, and dolls in long flowing prairie dresses in the glass window displays.

I wonder who buys these things and whether any modern kid actually appreciates the toys of old, but when I peek in through the window, I see that out back, they have the usual favorites like Lego sets, fire trucks, and LOL dolls. The pizza shop is located almost in the center, right next to one of the many Quail Lake gift shops, featuring stuffed bears, oversized T-shirts, thick socks, flip-flops, and other things that a visitor might have forgotten or might want to buy for friends back home.

I can smell the crust baking from the street and in front, a nice script. It says that all of the ingredients are fresh and the pizza is baked on site. My mouth starts to water, and I decide to get a slice while I'm there. I put in an order for a margarita and an iced tea, and then I show the clerk a picture of Sarah. She says that she doesn't know her and has never seen her but she had been off for a couple of days.

"Carlene!" the seventeen-year-old yells toward the back of the restaurant, and a plump middle-aged woman with a wide smile and a dirty white apron emerges, sticking her head out from the back.

"Can I help you?" she asks.

I fill her in and show her the picture on my phone.

She looks at it carefully, nods, wipes her hands on her apron, and then yells back, "Jack, I'll be back in a minute!" She walks closer to me, pulling me toward the refrigerated drink section near the empty booths.

"She was here that day," Carlene says, "with a guy. I don't know either of their names, and I haven't seen them before."

I pull up a picture of Dominic and she nods with approval. "Yes, that's him. They got a few slices and sat down at that booth over there." She points to the one in the corner, looking out onto the lake. "Cooing and awing at each other and sat on the same side of the booth, so I knew it was a date."

"What time was this? Afternoon?"

"They were the only ones here. It's our slow time, two to four o'clock."

"Okay. Do you know what happened afterward? Where they could have gone, or did anything unusual happen while they were here?"

"No, but what do you mean by unusual?"

"Did they get into a fight? Did he say something to her?"

"No, they were really happy with each other. I went out back, saw them kissing by the bathrooms, and I overheard them talking about going to a motel."

"Really?" My mouth drops open.

She nods. "Yes. I thought that they looked young for that, probably not even eighteen, but if the kids want some privacy, it probably is good to have a place to go."

I bite my lower lip and look around. "Do you have any idea what motel?"

She shakes her head. "No. Listen, I've got to get back."

Just at that moment, the guy from the kitchen yells her name.

"He can't be in there by himself. He's just started. He doesn't know what he's doing." She rolls her eyes and gives me a nod.

"Do you have any cameras around here?" I ask.

"No. I'm here all the time, a control freak in that way. My niece and I are the only ones working the cash register."

I thank her again for her time, go back to my booth, and finish my pizza.

Dominic had lied.

As I take big chunks, chewing generously to enjoy every fresh recently-baked bite, I review what Dominic had told me in my head. At no point did he mention that they went to a motel. So far, I'd had to pull all the information I'd gotten out of him with a lot of labor and force. That means that there's more to his story than he's letting on.

While I finish my iced tea, I start making calls. I compile a list of motels in town that they could have possibly gone to. There are six. Two on the outskirts, four closer in town. Of course, this doesn't take into account any number of Airbnbs and Vrbos that they could have also patronized. But those would be harder to book so last minute. I get a refill of the iced tea, plop it into my cupholder in the car, and start making the rounds. The first one is Motel 6, a little bit away from the lake.

When I check their names with the front desk clerk, they don't show up as being registered that day. It occurs to me that they could have used a fake name, but when I ask her about the registration process, she assures me that they require everyone to have a credit card. In case there's any damage or any other incidentals, the credit card has to be registered to a real name. I check the second hotel, a beautiful, restored bed and breakfast on the other side of the lake. The woman who owns it runs it with her son, and she also assures me that neither Dominic nor Sarah stayed at their hotel as a credit card matching the driver's license is required for booking a room.

The Wagon Wheel, a rustic two-story motel near Front Street, walking distance to the lake is my third stop. It has an enormous wagon wheel out front. A big and hand-carved cow skull head decorated in a Southwestern style is hanging at the entrance.

The rooms look simple, modest, but nevertheless, leaning into the Western theme with burlap window treatments, turquoise paintings inside the small lobby, and a small collection of jewelry and mountain town artifacts that are available for sale near the front desk. The clerk has a small name tag with the name "Nick" on it. He is maybe a nineteen, twenty, but weary, and dressed in jeans and a button-down shirt. When I lean over the counter, I see that he has a thick tome of old west tales called *The Old West True Stories, Myths, and Legends*, on the counter next to the laptop. I introduce myself, hand him my card, and show him pictures of Sarah and Dominic.

"Have you seen these two here by any chance?"

"Yes, a couple of days ago." He nods. "Can't remember exactly, but I think they came in the afternoon."

A small smile forms at the corner of my lips. Finally.

Now I have to make sure that the dates line up. I ask him to confirm with his records and give him their full names. Sarah's doesn't show up, and I give up a little bit and exhale a little bit of hope. When he searches Dominic's name, he taps on the screen with the end of his pencil and flashes his pearly whites, the kind that looks like they have never been exposed to black coffee.

"Yes. He registered here that day at three o'clock."

"Okay." I nod. "Good. Okay, good."

I write it down in my small notebook.

"Any chance you have any cameras set up around here?"

"Yes, of course," he says quickly, taking me by surprise.

"Don't look so shocked; we're going with the whole old west theme, but we have to have some cameras because we're dealing with modern-day thieves."

"That's good to hear."

"You'd be surprised how many people don't have that philosophy." He shrugs. "See that sign over there."

It's a small sticker attached to the glass, written in the type of script they used to use on wanted posters in the late 1800s.

"Carson means every word of it. Anyone caught stealing will be prosecuted to the fullest extent of the law. We had this one kid, early twenties, steal a TV from the room. His mistake was well, one, it was an old TV, the ones from the late '90s. Then it was so big it would barely fit into his hatchback, and he was a local boy. Carson put his picture in the community message boards and social media.

"Lo and behold, they found him at the airport. Got a job pumping gas in small private Cessnas. Didn't have that for long because Carson pressed charges and they went to court and all. Got it on his record."

"Carson seems like a tough boss. Is he around?" I ask. "I've met him before, working another case and it would be nice to say hello."

"No. He's down the hill getting some supplies today, but I can tell him you stopped by."

"Please do."

He looks down at my card in his hand and repeats my name, this time probably remembering it.

Nick checks the cameras for the date and time, focusing on room five.

"Wow, you have them actually positioned to each of the rooms?"

"Yeah." He nods. "After the incident with the TV, it was the best way. It's not that expensive to get a few cameras. Better to be safe than sorry."

He shows me Dominic and Sarah coming in and leaving an hour and forty-five minutes later. We check the parking lot out front and I see that they have come on bikes. The one that I know belongs to Sarah and the one that I had seen with Dominic are dropped right outside and locked up by one of the streetlights.

"Okay. This gives me a lot to go on."

I write down the dates and times, take a few pictures and videos of the recordings, and forward the copies of the video to my work email directly from Nick's computer.

With all this additional information to go on, Dominic and I have to have another chat.

16

CHARLOTTE

I get back to our rental cabin on the lake carrying a box of pizza to make amends to Dylan. As far as pizza goes, it's good enough for most apologies, but not one this big. This was supposed to be Dylan's and my weekend away after some difficult times. Given what happened with the fire, this was supposed to be a reprieve from work, from hassle, from everything else. But here I am spending it working a case. I find him on the porch, reading a thriller in the rocking chair, looking out onto the lake.

"How are you?" I ask, tiptoeing slightly toward him, handing him an apology.

"I had a good day." He smiles. "Went for a little dip, got some reading done, and took a nap. Watched some YouTube videos. Now out here about to enjoy the sunset."

"Yes, I know it's really late," I admit. "I'm sorry. There was just nothing I could really do. I had to do all the interviews one by one to try to get to the bottom of this. This is the first forty-eight hours."

"I know all of that, except that you probably don't even have jurisdiction up here."

"I do. In fact, Lieutenant Soderman asked me to step in. They're really short-staffed. This is still Mesquite County. My hands are tied."

"There's a deputy here who's available to do the majority of the work," Dylan says. "You know that as well as I do. You just don't trust him to do it."

"A girl has been murdered. I can't just let that go."

"It's not your case, Charlotte." He stands up and raises his voice. This has rarely-- no, in fact, this has never happened before. He narrows his eyes, and I can tell the frustration is boiling over within him. "Look, I don't ask you for much, but these hours, they're long."

"I know." I nod.

"It just doesn't feel like I'm much of a priority to you and I want to be."

"You are a priority, absolutely. Cases just come when they come. I don't have control over it. You, of all people, should know that."

"I do. Unfortunately." He nods. "I just thought that maybe there was something that you could do."

"Like what?" I snap. "What do you want me to do? Just leave this case to Gavin Skeeter? He's well-meaning but he's a Boy Scout. He has two years on the job maybe and he'd believe almost any story anyone tells him."

"He may rise to the occasion."

"Maybe, and if he doesn't, if he messes up the case--"

"You can't be everywhere and be everything to everyone."

"I'm not trying to be. I'm just trying to figure out what happened to Sarah Dunn. The thing is that I'm very close. I found out that Dominic, the guy that she had a crush on, the guy that she had snuck out and spent the whole afternoon with, lied about going to a motel room with her. What if something happened there? What if he went too far or maybe they slept together and that she had regrets? I have a feeling he's involved with this, and I can actually find out what happened unlike all of those cases that I have worked on in the past."

"Fine," Dylan says. "You do what you want to do, okay? I'm going to stay out of it."

"What is that supposed to mean?"

"Well, I'm going to continue enjoying my weekend in the mountains, with or without you. Want to work this case? Go ahead. I'm going to do what I want to do."

"I'm here now," I say.

"Well, I'm busy now." He stands up and walks away.

I can see the slight limp in his walk. It used to be much more pronounced, but he's trying to walk normally, despite the pain from the burns.

"You don't have to leave," I say. "I came back here to be with you, to spend some time together."

"Like I said, Charlotte, I'm not going to just wait around for you." Still holding onto his book, he walks down the stairs with a bit of difficulty and heads toward the lake.

I'm tempted to follow him, but I don't. I just sit down in the rocking chair and watch him walk away.

Uncertain as to where to go from here, I hang around for a bit, put the pizza in the fridge, watch the TV nervously, and then grab the car keys and head back to camp. If Dylan doesn't want to spend time with me, I'm not going to waste more of it waiting around either.

I want to talk to Dominic, get his story straight, and confront him about what I had heard. I head back to camp and call Gavin on the way there. He's still with Dr. Abbott. Bennett and Elizabeth are getting frustrated and annoyed since they are being kept from returning to their cabins. When I meet up with him, we make a plan. I tell him what I found out and that I am zeroing in on Dominic, but perhaps letting the girls go and having the rumor swirl around a little bit will be something that will be in our favor after all.

"Now that I have somewhat of a starting point, if we hear them talking, they might say something where someone might overhear them talking," I say. "If they won't come forward to us, they may talk to campers or their friends and we can get the information that way."

He gives me a shrug and a nod of approval. He doesn't give me much pushback giving evidence as to why I had my doubts about him. It's not that I don't think I'm right in the situation, I do. It's more that I wish that Dylan was here to overhear our conversation somewhat and to see just how little experience Deputy Gavin Skeeter has in all of this. I tell him to let the girls know and update Dr. Abbott about the situation. Then I ask him about Dominic and his whereabouts.

I FIND Dominic in his cabin joking around with his three roommates. I can hear them through the door right before I knock. When someone says, "Come in," I find them in various states of disarray around the room. A redheaded guy is climbing up to the top of the bunk, the guy with thick bushy hair is rushing after him, and Dominic is holding up something high in the air, a letter perhaps, that the smallest kid in the cabin is trying to reach. In none of their faces do I register any sort of fear or discomfort, just the usual tomfoolery among late adolescents. As soon as Dominic sees me, the smile on his face drops out of sight and he clenches his jaw, hands his roommate the letter, crosses his arms, and tells me that he has no interest in talking to me.

"Dominic, I need your help. There's been a development."

"What's she talking about?" one of them whispers.

"My name is Detective Charlotte Pierce," I repeat myself, hoping that they're listening more attentively now. "One of your camp counselors is gone. Sarah Dunn. I want to have a word with Dylan about the statement that he made, and I'm interested in speaking to the rest of you as well."

It occurs to me for a moment that I should have probably interviewed them earlier especially now that they're going to be on alert, but luckily Gavin is right behind me. I pull him aside for a moment when we step onto the porch and tell him that I want him to stay in the cabin with the guys to make sure that they don't work out a story about where they were, just in case they were at all involved in any of this.

"Do you really think they were?"

"I have no idea. As you know, Dominic has told me a lot of lies and I intend to question him about all of that. In terms of everything else, I don't know."

While Gavin stays with the boys, I pull Dominic outside.

"What? What do you want?" he snaps.

"I found out something about what you actually did that afternoon, Dominic, and I'm not happy, to tell you the truth."

Of course, I wish that this conversation was being recorded on something other than my phone, but it will have to do for now since a station and interview room are not exactly available.

"What do you want from me? I told you the truth."

"You did? Are you sure about that because I talked to the people at the Wagon Wheel Motel and they showed me that you were registered there that afternoon, and then they showed me the video of the two of you going into room number five and emerging about an hour and forty-five minutes later. Now, can you tell me what happened in that room, Dominic?"

"Nothing, nothing happened in that room."

"Are you sure about that?"

"Of course, I am."

"The way you were sure that nothing happened after the pizza shop?"

"Look, she didn't want anyone to know. Okay? We fooled around a little bit. Made out on the bed. I'm not going to go into the details of my sex life with some stranger."

"I'm not some stranger, Dominic. I'm a detective investigating her murder."

"Do I need a lawyer or something here?" he asks the magic words.

I clench my jaw. I have pushed him too much.

If he lawyers up now and says nothing, I only have the physical evidence, but no confession.

Confessions are not necessary, but very helpful. They go a long way in convincing the jury about what had happened one way or another. Sometimes even convincing them of things that didn't really occur. But this case is different. Dominic had something to do with her murder. What exactly, I do not know.

He paces back and forth on the porch, occasionally looking back at me.

Dominic slumps his shoulders and cracks his knuckles, his nerves flooding to the surface. When he swallows, I watch his Adam's apple move up and down in his throat.

"Listen, I'm here to help you. Just like I said before, but I need you to tell me the truth. You have been lying to me at every turn and that makes it very difficult for me to trust you."

"I don't need you to trust me," he snaps. "I had nothing to do with this."

"I have to tell you that right now, it looks like you did. You have lied to me on numerous occasions about your involvement with Sarah and then I find evidence that you kissed her at the pizza parlor. You guys got a motel room together. It doesn't look good."

"I dropped her off at camp and I haven't seen her since. Didn't her roommates say that they saw her that morning?"

"Yes, but roommates can be convinced to lie. Are you certain that alibi's going to hold up? When they think that you were actually involved in their friend's murder, do you think they're going to keep covering for you? I haven't told them yet that you went to the motel room together. They don't know anything about that."

He clenches his jaw again. I'm making him uncomfortable and that's exactly where I want him to be.

"I don't know what you want from me," Dominic says.

"I want you to tell me the truth."

I PRESS Dominic more and more as we stand on the porch and soon he starts to crack. At first, it's a physical thing. He gets flustered and emotional but he doesn't say a word.

Then, finally, he adds, "I didn't want to tell you because I didn't want Misty to find out. We just broke up. I wasn't sure how she would react to me going to a motel room with someone else. Actually, I knew exactly how she'd react. She'd be furious, and I didn't want her to be."

"Do you want to get back together with Misty?" I ask.

He shakes his head.

"No, I actually like Sarah a lot. Liked, I guess. I still can't believe that she's dead," he adds, shaking his head. "Are you sure that she's dead?"

I nod, looking him straight in the eye.

"She is, and I'm here to find out what happened. If there was an accident of any sort; maybe you did something you didn't mean to do. You know you can tell me that, right?"

I say that as sincerely as possible. I need him to trust me, but the truth is that he shouldn't. The accident, the possible explanation, placing yourself at the scene of what had happened is an approach to getting a confession. The person might have done it; he's not ready to admit what fully happened but he's ready to explain, to say that it was an accident. It's a way in. I expect Dominic to take the bait, but he doesn't.

"I told you what happened. We left the motel and came back here."

"Can anyone vouch for that?"

"My friends," he says. "Well, they were at dinner, but I joined them there."

"You went to dinner after you got pizza?"

"I was hungry after--" He pauses for a moment. "We fooled around for a little bit."

"How extensive was this exactly? I need to know if you had sex, if you kissed. How far did it go?"

"That's none of your business," Dominic says. "I have to go back and I don't want to answer any more of your questions."

"Dominic."

"Please, just leave me alone. Otherwise, I'm just going to call a lawyer because you're harassing me."

"That's not how a lawyer works."

"I don't have to answer any of your questions if I don't want to, right?"

He puts me in a bind. Now, it's my turn to clench my jaw.

"That's what I thought." He smiles. "I'm not going to answer any more of your questions, and you can't make me. If you want to arrest me, arrest me. That's what I thought," he adds after I don't make a move to read him his rights.

"You're making a mistake, Dominic."

"No, I don't think I am," he says, walks inside, and slams the door shut in my face.

17

CHARLOTTE

Gavin pokes his head out for a moment looking for guidance.

"We have to talk to everyone. Get everybody's statements," I say.

I try to think about the logistics of pulling three of the guys apart since there are only two of us and we don't exactly have a place to put them, but luckily Dr. Abbott shows up and I get his help.

"The main thing I want you to find out is what exactly Dominic was doing that night. Did they see him at dinner, earlier, later? Was he home that night?" I instruct Gavin.

I need him to do this for me. I plan to interview one of them as well but then my phone rings. The long-awaited call, the medical examiner. I had called her a few times already, left messages, but received nothing in return.

"Sorry, I've got a lot of stuff going on here," she says, sounding frazzled on the other end. "It's what you suspected, though. Preliminary findings, strangulation marks around the neck, bruises on the body. Most self-inflicted, however."

"That's what I suspected," I say. "She cut herself a bit. I saw that. Any new bruises?"

"Some. She fought hard for her life. Unfortunately, it wasn't enough."

"Anything else?" I ask after a brief pause. I can hear a click of her tongue as she looks at the paperwork.

"There was no blood. There were no fluids or water in her lungs. No signs of a sexual encounter. She didn't drown. No, whoever did this didn't push her head underwater. Looking at the rest of the crime scene, it's possible that they transferred her body over there, but I can't be too sure."

"What about her fingernails? The DNA."

"That's going to take a while."

"You're kidding me."

"The state lab is backed up. I prioritized this as much as I could and it's marked a high priority, there's still an order to which the technicians can get to it, and there's a long line. There are, of course, private labs but that's going to depend on the budget of the county and whether the lieutenant approves it."

I grumble for a moment, but eventually acquiesce and ask her to let me know as soon as she hears something. I'm about to ask her about her personal life and her kid, but she says that she has to go. She has other calls to make and she's trying to get home at a reasonable time today.

Armed with the results, with the video from the motel, my suspicions about Dominic, I make the call to Lieutenant Soderman with an update. He listens carefully, chomping on a sandwich in the background. I call him at home as he's still recovering, but he takes calls anytime until ten or eleven at night. I update him on everything, and he sounds positive, in a good mood. I wish I had something else to butter him up with because what I'm going to ask him is going to be vague.

"We're not going to be able to get the DNA from the state lab for a while," I say, "but I was hoping that you could find room in the budget to send this to a private lab."

He takes a pause from chewing, then swallows.

"Lieutenant?"

"I don't think we can do that, Charlotte," he says with disappointment in his voice.

"Are you sure? Maybe there's something we can do." I can hear him shaking his head on the other end.

"Unfortunately not. We just have to wait until we get the free results, but it could be weeks. Well, this kid, Dominic, is still going to be at camp, right? Unless you scared him off."

"No, I mean, he was pretty mad, but I don't think he's going anywhere; he seems to be pretty cocky."

"I'd love to help you out, Charlotte, but the budget is tight. There've been cutbacks. We're pretty short-staffed as is, and we need to spend what we can on new deputies. You know that."

I keep trying to get my point across to the lieutenant, but he doesn't seem to understand the urgency. At the end, he gets quite short and tells me that the conversation is over.

"Listen, from what you told me, it looks like this case could be solved with a confession," Lieutenant Soderman says. "Now, why don't you go out there and do that before the DNA evidence comes back?"

18

CHARLOTTE

I pace back and forth, angry at myself for the phone call. Perhaps there was something I could have done, a different approach I could have taken, except that, of course, there isn't. You can't get blood from a stone, and if there is no money, then what exactly is the option? There isn't one. Lieutenant Soderman is absolutely right. My only choice here is to wait on the DNA evidence and to try to elicit a confession.

My phone rings, and without looking at the screen, I answer, thinking that it's the lieutenant calling me back. "Hey, thanks for getting back to me," I say.

"You didn't call me," the man on the other end says, and I realize that it's Will.

"Oh, sorry. I thought that you were someone else."

"You don't sound so excited to hear from me."

I can feel the smile on his face on the other end.

"Listen, I have to tell you something," he says, suddenly pivoting to a much more serious discussion. "Erin's in the hospital. She almost lost the baby. They have her on all these tubes, and I'm just freaking out."

"Oh my God. I'm so sorry."

"What if something happens?"

"Nothing is going to happen. They have her stabilized, right?"

"Yes, for now."

"How far along is she?"

"Five months," he says, without missing a beat.

"It's going to be okay, Will," I lie, asking him for more details.

"She just started having these cramps and there was a bit of blood. She wanted to go to the hospital, and that's what we did. I was telling her the whole time that she's overreacting, but she was right."

Will is an old partner of mine, and an old friend. He was the one person in the department who I trusted unconditionally, and thought that I could depend on.

Not that anyone else is particularly suspicious, but he and I were close. He got my jokes, has a similar sense of humor, and hearing him like this, broken and lost, is difficult. What's even more difficult is working cases without him by my side.

"How is she doing now?" I ask.

"Fine, I guess. They have her stabilized. They're watching her very carefully and she has to stay in bed. They're not sure if they'll be able to discharge her anytime soon, and if they do, then they said that she has to remain on bed rest."

"Oh, man, that really sucks."

"I just hope, more than anything, that we don't lose this baby."

"Me, too. Is there anything I can do?"

There's a long pause on the other end.

"Life has been really crappy, Charlotte, ever since--"

His voice drops off. He doesn't want to talk about it and neither do I.

He and Erin were childhood loves. They reconnected when she came back to town, and they started up a relationship when she was going through stuff with her ex-husband, who ended up being found dead with his new wife in their house. Because Erin was cyberstalking them and following their every move, not to mention that she was in their house with very little memory about how she got there, she became a primary suspect.

The problem is that you can't be an investigator working a case if you're also romantically linked to the primary suspect. I found out about him and Erin later, but I knew enough to know it was improper. We however did nothing but follow the leads in the case. The leads showed that it was someone else altogether who had killed her ex-husband, his wife, and their unborn child.

The problem was that while you can make an arrest, you have to make it stick in court, and that's a much harder sell. The defense attorney hired private investigators and they uncovered what Will wasn't exactly hiding, mostly because he didn't want to make it look like he was committing fraud at all. They followed Erin to one of her medical appointments and discovered that he was there, the soon-to-be father of her baby.

"Listen, don't worry about anything with the mistrial or any of the legalities of anything that's going on," I urge him. "I want you to just focus on helping Erin get through this and keeping your family together and as healthy as possible."

"There's nothing else I really can do," he says. "I'm just here at the hospital."

"I wish I could be there for you right now, but I can't. I'm working this case up in Quail Lake."

"Yes, I know," he says. "Lieutenant told me."

"I need you so much up here. Your point of view, your ability to check on my work. I'm floundering."

"Any chance I can help out?"

I shrug. "I wish you could, but you're officially on leave from the department, right?"

"Yes. Internal Affairs is investigating everything and I'm off for now."

I urge him again to keep his head high.

"What's happening with the mistrial? Is it officially going forward?" he asks.

"Yes. The ADA couldn't stop it. You're going to have to gather other evidence to make that case stick, or they're probably going to assign it to other detectives. Who knows?"

"What other evidence is there? What about what happened at the end? That has to mean something."

"You'd think so, but it's all fruit of the poisonous tree, as you know. We wouldn't have been there if we hadn't suspected them. We wouldn't have suspected them if we hadn't turned our attention from Erin. We can try to argue inevitable discovery, but I don't know if anyone will buy it."

"God, I wish I could have some work to keep me busy right now. I'm crawling up the walls here."

"Yes, but I don't know, why don't you just try to distract yourself with something else, a hobby, anything you like to watch on TV?"

"Not a lot of sports on at nine in the morning. Not a lot of sports on right now in the dead of summer," he says.

"That was just something to look forward to. You need some hobbies, Will," I say.

"Hey, when did you stop calling me Torch?" he asks after a moment. It's a nickname that I used to use.

I shrug my shoulders. "It's been a while. Ever since you became a friend, more than a colleague."

"I like it."

I urge him again to stay strong, to be there for Erin, and he promises that he will.

"I can always do some fantasy football, right? On my phone. Maybe play a few rounds of poker. Online casinos are open."

"Yes, but don't lose too much money, otherwise, Erin's going to not let you live it down."

"Good point." He laughs, and I see Gavin standing at the end of the porch, looking at me like he has something important to tell me.

19

CHARLOTTE

I meet with Misty Copeland in the evening. It's getting late and she's about to go to bed, dressed in an oversized T-shirt and pajama shorts. Her hair is long and wet from a recent shower. Her face is a little bit sunburnt from the day. She steps out onto the porch of her cabin, putting her finger in front of her mouth to indicate that her roommates are sleeping.

"Two of them are training for a marathon, so they go to bed really early," she says.

"How about you?" I ask.

"I don't stay up too late, but no eight o'clock bedtime for me either. It's a good thing I have my phone and iPad to pass the evenings when I'm not out."

I get the sense that she's friendly enough with her roommates and somewhat willing to talk to me. She's aware of Sarah's disappearance, but not more than that, from the fact that her birthday party was canceled.

"How close were you with Sarah?"

"Not really," she admits. "I saw her here and there. We weren't assigned to any of the same jobs. You think that this camp would be big enough, but you don't end up making friends with every single person."

"Did you ever talk to her?"

"Yes. I think we had breakfast a few times, just in a big group, maybe exchanged pleasantries, but nothing else."

I give her a slight nod. I don't have my notepad out because I want to make this a casual stop-by kind of conversation. Take some of the pressure off and not put her on her back foot. I turn my questioning. It doesn't take me long to bring up Dominic. That's really what I'm here for.

"Can I ask you about your relationship with Dominic Marcel?"

"We dated. We started dating at the last week of camp last year. We knew each other all last summer and the summers before. We were counselors together and then campers before that. I really liked him. We tried to get this long-distance thing to work, but it was hard. There were jealousies involved. I'd call and then he wouldn't answer. He'd call and I'd be out. We FaceTimed a lot initially, but it was hard to see each other. We live three hours away, and my mom doesn't let me drive that far by myself."

"What about him? Did he come see you?"

"Yes, a few times. My mom let him sleep over at our house a few times, in separate rooms and all. When I came to visit him for the day, his family was around. It was just complicated, and we're teenagers, right? We're not supposed to be married."

"Yes, I understand. Is there anything else you can tell me?"

She looks down at her feet, shifting her weight from one foot to the other. Something about this conversation is making her very nervous.

"Why are you interviewing me? Do you think that Dominic had something to do with Sarah's disappearance?"

The way she pauses to say disappearance makes me think twice. "What's wrong? You don't believe that she disappeared?" I ask.

"No. Of course, I do. It's just that she's dead, right?"

I lick my lips and suddenly realize just how chapped they are and how dry my mouth is. I have a bottle of water back in the car, but moments like this in conversations are important to capture. They reveal so much about the person, the character. This is the first time that she's admitted that she knows that Sarah's dead. Is there any significance to that, I wonder?

"How do you know that she is dead?"

"I heard that from a few people. The rumors are flying around. You're here, talking to people, interviewing her roommates, Dominic, his roommates."

"Oh, you heard about that?"

"One of his roommates texted my roommate. They're in a group chat together. They do canoeing. Rumors spread really fast around here, and the truth, probably even faster."

She pulls her hair up into a tight bun on top of her head. She has almond eyes, olive skin, and a pouty little mouth that I'm sure makes her quite popular in school, but she doesn't have an attitude the way that Elizabeth does. She seems to have an easygoing kind of approach to life that naturally puts people at ease as well.

"She's dead, right?"

"Yes, she is," I confirm, largely because I want her to tell her roommates and to tell Dominic's roommates. I hope that they watch him and question him about it and maybe he'll crack. Maybe he'll share something with his friends that he wouldn't share with a stranger, let alone an investigator.

"Did she kill herself?" Misty asks.

She looks up at me through her lashes, not really tilting the rest of her head up.

"Why would you say that?"

"Because she joked about it."

"She did?"

"I don't know, she had a few marks on her arms and legs. She admired all these musicians who had killed themselves or overdosed. She loved movies about death and autopsies. She liked true crime, too, but that doesn't exactly make her that special. Who doesn't love to fall asleep to some dark *Dateline* kind of stories, right?"

"I gather you do?" I ask.

She nods. "Many of us do. They're scary stories for adults, aren't they? Something to keep you up at night, a warning about what will happen if you make mistakes, date the wrong guy."

"You think that dating the wrong guy warrants you getting killed?"

"No, of course not. That's why at the end they always get justice or almost always. I don't like the ones about the open-ended mysteries, still missing, unsolved crimes. My roommate is all about that, but I can't handle it. I need certainty in my life, especially when it comes to entertainment."

I can tell by the way she speaks and the clarity of her statement that she's a pretty smart teenager, self-aware as well. That doesn't mean that she can't be tripped up to admit something that she shouldn't if I set the stage for that.

"Tell me about you and Dominic some more," I ask. "He said you wrote him a letter."

"He told you that?" Her cheeks flush red.

"Well, not exactly, but I heard that around."

"I didn't want to be with him anymore. I met this guy at school. We hooked up. I felt bad about it, but it happened. I didn't want to tell him that I cheated on him, and so I thought it'd be kinder to just tell him that I don't want to be with him anymore."

"Is that kinder?" I ask.

"I don't know. People talk about closure or whatever, but how does him feeling crappy about himself and knowing that I cheated on him make anything better? The truth was that I didn't want to do it. I didn't want to have this long-distance relationship."

"You weren't going to be long distance anymore, right?" I ask.

"No. It was a week before camp was supposed to start, but it was still too much. He had been mean to me, yelled at me for not answering his calls, texting him back. He was getting obsessive. I was possessive earlier when I was feeling insecure, but then I just stopped caring. I don't know why I need to explain all this stuff. I didn't want to date him anymore and so I didn't."

"No, you're right. Absolutely. I'm just trying to figure out what could have happened to Sarah exactly."

"What does my relationship with Dominic have to do with that?"

"He was with her the day before."

Misty looks up at me and takes a step back as if I had delivered a blow. She had, apparently, not known this.

"What do you mean?" she whispers.

"They met up at the dock," I say, "and then they had plans to skip out on work, and went to the pizza shop in town in the afternoon. They went thrifting, spent some time together."

"That was it?"

"And a motel," I add, watching her expression.

Her face practically contorts on itself. This was clearly something that Dominic didn't want her to know, but I need her to know this in order to gauge what she might or might not know about Dominic.

Is she covering up for him?

Does she actually know what he did, but he had lied about this? If that's the case, then perhaps she'll come forward and tell us something that he wants to keep hidden.

"Fine. I mean, we're broken up. He wasn't my boyfriend anymore, so why would I care about that?"

"And you don't?" I ask.

She shakes her head. "No."

"Are you sure?"

"Things didn't work out with this guy from school, okay? Now, Dominic and I are together all the time. I see him. I can't say that I don't miss him. We have a history. We never got to be together and it was stupid and impulsive for me to break up with him right before camp was just about to start. I should have just waited until we were here."

"Yes, except for the fact that the girl he went to a motel with is dead now, and I was just wondering what else you may know about that."

Misty narrows her eyes. It finally hits her.

"I had nothing to do with her death."

"And what about Dominic?"

"I don't know." She shakes her head. "I mean, I would hope not but I have no idea."

She backs away from me and shuts down. I try again and again, but she doesn't respond. I know I need to give her some time to think, percolate, maybe even call Dominic on what he might have done.

20

CHARLOTTE

I spend a restless night at the cabin. Dylan is asleep by the time I get back, and this trip is going nothing like I thought it would.

Instead of hand-in-hand walks in the moonlight along the lake and making love after dinner, I'm spending my time with an inexperienced deputy who is thankfully willing and hardworking, interviewing a bunch of kids about the murder of their friend.

I toss and turn throughout the night. The following morning I drag myself out of bed. Gavin calls me to the station, bribing me with coffee and doughnuts.

I'm tired and groggy, but the sugar does its job, perking me up momentarily.

The word station is quite an exaggeration. It is just a large office that's locked most of the time. No one goes there except for the people who have keys. It's not open to the public in any sense of the word. It's just the place where the deputies working up here can rest, leave their stuff, and stop by occasionally.

There are two long folding tables in an L-shape along the wall. I sit on one of the flimsy plastic chairs, chewing absentmindedly. There are two big windows looking out like storefronts.

I ask him whether this used to be a retail space before the county took it over.

He nods.

"Yes, apparently, we got a good rate on it, and that's why we got a station at all. I mean, we needed it, somewhere that isn't someone's house, to get together and conduct some sort of interviews or even just do paperwork. Otherwise, it is a pretty remote job. I mean, I took the county-issued vehicle to my house and filled out paperwork at home."

"You know, that doesn't sound too terrible," I say, trying to imagine what it'd be like to do everything at the house versus at the station back down in the valley.

"At least you can get into your pajamas and just zone out, right?" I smile.

I eat half of a glazed doughnut after cutting it with a knife and then grab one with sprinkles. Gavin looks nervous, but it takes me a little bit to even notice. "What's going on?" I ask him.

He has a manila folder in front of him. I feel like he's going to ask me to co-sign for a loan. He doesn't. Instead, he just opens it up, shuffles the papers, and closes it again.

"Gavin, you can tell me anything. This is what we're here for. Did you find out something about the case?"

"Well, kind of. It's just a possibility, but I think it's a little stupid."

"There's nothing stupid. I mean, the case is wide open. Go ahead."

"There was a drifter," he says.

There's a flake of frosting or powder around the corner of his lips, and I touch mine to point to it. He wipes it with his thumb and shows me his notes, which are unreadable.

"Can you just sum up? This looks like it was written by a cardiologist."

He makes a frowny face knowing that I'm just making fun of him, and I'm glad that we've gotten this far in our relationship to make these kinds of jokes.

"I don't know if it's anything," he says.

"That's not how you start out cases. You start out making statements if you want to convince somebody."

"I'm not even trying to convince you. I'm just trying to state the facts here."

"Okay, go ahead. I'm listening."

I bite into the sprinkles once again and savor them on my tongue for a moment before inhaling another two bites.

"A couple of the campers told me that they saw some guy on the perimeter. When I talked to Misty before you talked to her, she mentioned him."

"Wait, you talked to her before I did?" I ask.

He shrugs. "I didn't tell her anything. Just asked if there was anything suspicious that she had seen anywhere at camp. Very generic. I talked to a bunch of kids at the same time. It's not like I isolated her or anything like that."

"Okay, go on."

"Dr. Abbott had mentioned it to me. When I was talking to him when you were doing the other interviews, he had brought it up. There was just this man that no one knew of. A few people thought that he was doing some cleanup work or something like that, but he was seen in and out of the property."

"Do you have a description?"

"Yes. White male, mid-forties, brown hair, square jaw. One of the art teachers felt uncomfortable with him while they were painting outside, so she asked him to leave."

"A number of people noticed him?"

"Seems like it." Gavin nods.

"Did anyone make any calls to the police or anything like that?"

"It never got that bad. As soon as anyone made any eye contact with him, he just stomped off. It's probably one of the reasons why some people thought it was the maintenance crew."

"Were all the maintenance people identified? Did you see all of them there?"

"Yes. Dr. Abbott introduced us, and he knows everyone, so he wasn't one of those people, but it was the campers who saw him that thought he was there working on something."

"Was he wearing a work shirt? Why would they think that?"

"He was dressed a little bit like the gardening guy. Not a work shirt per se but the khaki pants and a shirt that seems to be popular."

Feeling adequately stuffed with delicious doughnuts, I finish my coffee and look up at him. Gavin looks lost. I pull out his manila folder, looking through the papers. He had written up each individual interview with each individual camper, teacher, and Dr. Abbott on a separate report sheet by hand.

"I'm going to type these up soon. I just haven't had time to get their signatures yet, but I wanted to have them ready for you in case you wanted to read the reports."

"These look good, Gavin. Did you work on this all last night?"

"I thought that the sooner that I can get on this the better."

"You're right. I'm suddenly feeling like the drifter angle is really complicating an otherwise non-complicated case."

"You're not happy about this?" Gavin asks, his eagerness waning a little bit.

He seems so eager to please, but I can tell that he also doesn't want to be perceived to be doing anything wrong.

"It's nothing about you, Gavin, or your police work. Trust me. This is great. I'm glad you talked to all those people, and you got these statements. This definitely could be something. I mean, a guy watching a bunch of pre-teens and teenagers at camp? That's a little odd, but—"

He finishes my thought for me, "But I don't know if it means anything. You know more than I do. So, what do you think happened?"

"I'm leaning toward Dominic. He lied about being with her at first. He lied about going to a motel with her. Who knows what else he lied about? There is the problem in that her roommates said that they all saw her in the morning, but they might be helping him out some way. When I talked to Misty, his ex-girlfriend, I let it slip that they stayed in the motel together, and she was pissed off, to say the least, more like shocked but hurt, all of those things. She had no idea. Either that or she's an amazing actress."

"You told her?"

"Yes, I told her that to push her buttons. Now that people know that Sarah was killed, I want him to talk to his friends. They're going to have a lot of questions. I want his ex-girlfriend to go and talk to him, too. Maybe he'll let something slip to them that he wouldn't tell us. Something interesting, something on point."

Gavin smiled. "Yes, it's probably him. So, the thing is that the drifter, this person that all these people saw, complicates the story, but we're not here to frame anybody. There's DNA evidence under her fingernails, so it's going to take a long time to test, unfortunately, since we have to use the free lab. That is going to confirm whether it was Dominic, this guy, or somebody else altogether."

"I'm glad that you got all these statements. You're very thorough. I appreciate that. It doesn't matter that it doesn't help my theory. Okay?"

He smiles.

"We're looking for evidence to lead us somewhere. We're not hypothesizing about something and then constructing the evidence to fit it, or at least we're trying not to do that. I want you to know that whoever you work with in the future, that's bad police work. If you see someone doing that, disregarding things that don't help their initial case, be on alert. Our goal here is not to arrest people and to give the cases to the prosecutor. Our goal here is to find out the truth and get justice for the victims. If it's not Dominic, then I want to know who it is. Okay?"

Gavin nods with enthusiasm. The pep talk seems to do both of us some good. Doing this long enough, you sometimes forget what your job is all about. You're so focused on eliciting confessions that you don't stop to think whether you're getting the right people to confess in the first place. I'm well aware of just how many false confessions the police get from people.

The truth is that it's much easier than we all want to admit. The pressure of the interrogation room, the person in a position of authority believing that you had done something wrong and threatening you with prison time. People will admit to a lot, even if it's a mistake. Sometimes they'll come forward and say that they did things that they never did in order to get on our good side, in hopes of convincing us that they had nothing to do with it.

People tend not to realize how fragile their minds can be in the right circumstances; how suggestible they are. They believe they would never say that they did something they didn't do. But we are not nearly as in control as we like to imagine. It is a frightening thought.

In fact, there are enough false confessions that I tend to side on getting rid of them altogether, at least using the techniques that most police departments currently use: any sort of pressure, any sort of lying. But then the rate of solved homicides will drop from fifty percent to under twenty. And we can't have that and be hard on crime, especially when the next election rolls around, and there's always the next election.

The truth is that there are not that many. TV programs would have you believe that every crime comes with a slew of evidence, DNA, blood, urine, the works, but the truth is that most of the time there's nothing. There are no video cameras. There's no DNA. There are no fingerprints. No casings, just a few bullet wounds, and that's it.

Luckily, in this case, we have more. We have people with stories to tell. In this case, a confession might work because they'll conflict with other stories that the person would tell their friends and colleagues, but if it's the drifter, if it's not Dominic, I don't know. Then the case can go cold and unsolved for a long time.

My phone rings and I glance at the screen. It's Sarah's mother calling again. I have been avoiding her calls all yesterday, but today, I don't know if I can do this anymore. I asked Gavin to fill in for me. I know that I'm asking the impossible. She's particularly volatile, upset, and he's a rookie, but I have other things to take care of today, and I hope that he can fill in.

"Okay, I'll talk to Mrs. Dunn," Gavin says, "but only if you do me a favor in return."

I tilt my head. He's learning how this game is played a little faster than I had anticipated. He tries to grab the napkins and the bags from the doughnuts to throw away, but I get there first.

"You got breakfast. I'll clean up." I smile. "Okay, what favor do you want?"

"Well, you know how Elizabeth knew that Sarah and Dominic went to the motel. I figured we haven't talked to her about it yet, really confronted her."

"Wait, what do you mean?" I ask, the gears in my head starting to move. "She *knew* about the motel?"

21

CHARLOTTE

The conversation this morning with Gavin has been beyond revelatory. The drifter angle is a clear possibility, but the one thing that I had no idea about was the fact that Elizabeth knew about Sarah's trip to the motel with Dominic.

How did Gavin find out? He said he had overheard her talking to her roommates while he was there during Dr. Abbott's announcement of Sarah's birthday party cancellation. For some reason he assumed that I knew all along, but how could I?

As soon as I give him Mrs. Dunn's number and tell him to put her at as much ease as possible and get more information from her about her relationship with Sarah, but don't tell her anything about any of our leads, I head straight to Elizabeth's cabin. It's after breakfast and no one's there. When I ask one of the campers where I can find her, she says archery.

Archery class takes place in the valley right before the beginning of the forest, a little bit past the lake and the crafts tables that do double-duty as picnic tables in the afternoons. Elizabeth shows the younger campers how to pull a bow slowly but let go of it quickly, not to keep the tension since your arm tends to start to shake and it's more difficult to hit the target. The campers are about ten to twelve years old, all a lot less coordinated than their counselor, but she's patient, elegant in her well-fitted T-shirt and tight shorts that accentuate her slim, model-like figure.

Her movements are slow and deliberate. For a moment there, it seems like she's almost floating on air. I watch from afar. It's after ten and due to the wind storm last night, the temperature has cooled off to the high sixties. It's going to be another perfect, mountain summer day in the books.

Elizabeth continues to help the campers, this time by letting them each shoot one arrow and watching them, studying them carefully with her arms crossed, peering at both their form and the target. Then she looks up over the ridge and spots me standing on the crest of the ridge. Her smile fades and she suddenly looks annoyed, frustrated, like she's resisting the temptation to roll her eyes. I can't watch in silence anymore. I have no choice but to head over and confront her.

As soon as I'm within earshot, she says loudly, "I can't talk now. We're busy."

"Yes, I can see that," I say. "I don't mind waiting."

"Well, I mind *you* waiting. You're distracting the kids and stressing me out."

"I really need to speak to you, Elizabeth."

"I already told you everything I know."

"This is about your roommate, isn't it?" a pudgier camper with rich auburn hair and freckles asks, gleeful at the gossip.

"My roommate is gone, and I already told the police everything I know."

"We need to review certain aspects of your statement," I say, trying to be as non-detailed as possible. "Why don't you finish your archery lesson and then we can talk?"

Rolling her eyes, she looks at her smart watch. "It's still twenty-five more minutes."

"I'll wait," I say and give them an adequate amount of space, but I don't retreat so far that she doesn't see me. Instead, I remain a presence for a while, waiting, not so much lurking but standing tall, being there as a reminder that she can't get away. Not that easily.

Finally, when the archery lesson is over and the campers start to head up the hill, Elizabeth collects the bows and arrows and puts them in their separate bins on the side.

"I have another lesson in ten minutes," she says, "so you better make this quick."

"I will. Why don't you tell me about what you know about Dominic and Sarah at the motel room?"

Her eyes get big for a moment. "I don't know anything about that."

"I think you do," I challenge her. "Someone overheard you talking to your roommate, so I have no problem asking them as well. You had words with Sarah. Can you tell me about that?"

I made up this part. It just sort of came out, in hopes of leading her somewhere.

"It wasn't a fight," she cracks, and I force back the smile that almost rises to my lips. I wasn't exactly sure if she'd admit it.

She could have easily gotten her roommates to stay on her side, but here she is coming forward, telling me something that would certainly be in her best interest to keep quiet.

"She shouldn't have gone to that motel room with him. If she wanted Dominic, she needed to make him wait. That's how boys are. If you give them what they want, if he sleeps with you on the first date, what's the point? I mean, why would they keep coming around?"

"Is that your approach to life and boys?" I ask.

"No, not exactly, but I've made some mistakes, so I was just trying to stop her from making the same ones."

"Is that what started it? Is that what you had a fight about?"

"Yes, she told me to mind my own business and that I had nothing to do with this."

"How did you find out about them going to the motel room?"

"She came back all giddy, excited, and she wasn't going to tell us at first, but then she did. She said that they kissed and much more in the room."

Okay, so she came back, I say silently to myself. Dominic was not the last person to see her, at least not in that motel room.

"She said I was jealous. She said that I wanted him or something stupid like that. Of course, I don't. I could have any guy I want, and if I wanted Dominic, then he would be mine."

"Did you tell her this?" I ask.

"Yes. Then she got all pissed, like she didn't know if that was completely true."

The delusion and self-involvement are difficult to process, but given how she looks at her age and the power that she wields with friends and guys, I get a sense of what she's actually like.

"I can imagine that Sarah wasn't too happy with that."

"No, she wasn't, but it's the truth; everyone knows that."

"Okay. Then what happened?"

"Nothing. We just had a fight. So what?"

Her phone rings. I see 'Mom' flash on the screen. She answers it before I can stop her. Then she mentions that I'm with her. My chest tightens. Her mom's voice gets elevated on the other end of the line. Suddenly, Elizabeth starts to cower. She disappears within herself. Her face turns pale, and the confidence and arrogance of the young woman at the height of her power, all but vanishes.

Still holding the phone which she places on speaker, she says, "My mom said that I can't talk to you anymore. I'm not going to be making anymore statements."

"Do you hear that?" her mom yells. "She's underage. You should know better. From now on you can only talk to us through our attorney."

The magic words have been spoken, but partly, I'm thankful. If she had admitted anything or any involvement whatsoever, her family would've brought up the fact that she's underage and she was questioned without an attorney present.

"That's fine," I say. "I was just asking a few questions. Your daughter is not a suspect. I was hoping she could provide some answers that might help me solve this case."

"I don't care," Elizabeth's mom snaps. "We'll answer all of your questions, but only through our attorney."

Elizabeth holds up her phone in my face as if it were a shield to get me to back off. I raise my hands up in defeat. She hasn't given me everything, but I'm walking away with a smile.

She has given me enough to go on, to ask others who might know more. After a few more stories and a few more pieces of evidence, I believe that no one's fancy attorney will be able to help them hide the truth.

22

CHARLOTTE

The following morning, it's hard to know how to proceed. What I need is time, time to put pressure on Elizabeth and others who might have been involved, time to find out the truth, time that I don't have.

But I'm here for a limited number of days. Every time I interact with Dylan, I realize that they are fleeting. I can't blame him exactly. He knows how difficult this is and how much pressure I'm under, but this is also supposed to be our time away.

If I were to stay the extra days and extend the trip, that would just pull me away from him. We end up being ships passing in the night. I wait for him to look busy to sneak out and I make excuses about where I'm going. I had made a promise to make it up to him and go to dinner, but I'm distracted with my attention elsewhere, and he feels it.

"You don't have to be here if you don't want to," he says with a sigh. His silence and discontent is showing more than he probably wants it to.

It is during one of these interactions filled with long pauses and awkward talks while we're grabbing a bite to eat at a local diner in town that I get a call from Kelsey Hall. It's a reprieve, an opportunity for me to think about something else, do something else.

I show him my phone in an effort to possibly explain that this time I'm being pulled away by an old case instead of this new one. He just shrugs and gives me a look of resignation that I'm getting uncomfortably accustomed to. I don't want to talk in the middle of the restaurant, no matter how small and quaint and how empty. I leave him alone with his phone for company and sneak out back.

The thunderstorms of early afternoon are rolling in. The ground starts to smell and gets filled with the scent of impending water. I feel the drench that's about to come down from the clouds. I've always loved the scent of a rainstorm in the summertime, breaking up the sun and the heat as the cloud cover comes in, but here it's particularly encouraging. The pine trees seem to almost turn inward into themselves as if to protect the overgrown forest floors.

"Hey, Kelsey, it's good to hear from you," I answer, clearing my throat and putting a peppy tone into it to make sure that she doesn't get a hint that anything is wrong.

"Are you okay?"

She doesn't buy it. We haven't seen each other in years and yet she seems to know everything there is to know about all of my overly friendly ways of being in the world, trying to make up for the inconvenience of having an actual mood.

"Yes. Just happy to hear from you," I lie.

She pauses for a moment as if giving me space to think about what I have just said.

"Listen, I'm going to Seattle. I've decided," she says.

"What do you mean?" I ask.

"I want to see my parents. I want to call them on who I am and the fact that they're not answering my calls and all of that."

"Really?"

"Yes. I was thinking of putting it off for a while, but I just can't. They're full of crap and they know it and I'm done putting up with it."

"What is going to happen?" I ask.

"I'm going to ask them all about it."

I can feel her smiling.

"I think I've waited long enough. I thought I would give them space, maybe give them an opportunity to collect their thoughts, but I don't owe them anything. I just figured I don't want to do that, so I'm not going to." I know this is a big step for her. I had brought this up before, but she wasn't ready. They had rejected meeting her, finding an explanation for what could have been the reason why the DNA didn't match.

"They know the truth," she says. "They know that it might be me, but they're still ignoring it. They're lying about something. I'm going to find out. They're dead to me anyway. I have nothing to lose."

"I think that's very brave of you," I say quietly.

Big fat raindrops begin to fall and hit against the windshield of a parked car. The sound they make is piercing, almost like hail. We talk about the rain up in the Northwest and how for years she had missed it with every fiber of her being, and then suddenly something happened, and she just didn't care anymore.

"For a long time, I thought of it as home every time it rained," she says. "I missed it desperately, but then I just knew that they wrote me off. It made me very sad."

"Is there any way that this could be a mistake?"

"One of them is lying about something," she says. "I don't know what exactly, but I'm going to find out. I just want to ask you one thing."

I nod, but don't respond.

"Are you there?"

I realize that she can't see me.

"Yes, of course," I say.

"Will you come with me?"

I walk back inside to the awkward dinner with Dylan, but suddenly, the awkwardness vanishes altogether.

"I'm going to go to Seattle with her," I say "It's the right thing to do. She needs my help."

"Yes, I understand."

He knows all about what's been going on with Kelsey, what I've done and not done, and the mistakes I've made. This is the least that I can do. He and I both know that. The fact that she's still willing to have me in her life means a lot. While some people believe that certain secrets should be taken to the grave, I don't, at least not when it comes to this one. If I can help her figure out what happened and help her get to the truth, then I would actually be worthy of the word friend.

23

CHARLOTTE

The dinner with Dylan ends on a high note, much to probably both of our surprise. We laugh and chat. The tension of me taking the phone call seems to somehow break up the conversation. I reassure him that I won't be going to Seattle until this case is solved, or at least becomes impossible to solve and reaches some sort of inevitable dead end, which at this point seems unlikely. This seems to perk him up and I fill him in on some of the details that I can freely share.

"Kelsey agreed to wait?" he asks.

I nod, taking a bite of my overdone sandwich, but enjoying the French fries off of his plate, nevertheless.

"One of these days someone's going to call you on stealing food from other people's plates. If you want some fries, you order yourself a side dish. The waiter clearly asked you whether that's something you wanted."

"I know, but I don't want the whole thing. I just want a few bites."

"At this rate you've had at least ten bites."

He accentuates the word looking straight into my eyes and I begin to laugh. He laughs as well and the mood lightens, allowing us to move on to less intense subjects, and at least for now, we avoid the conversation about the demands of my job. When we get back to the Airbnb, I plop down on the couch, but he grabs my hand and pulls me into his arms.

This is a nice surprise. I smile and kiss him with an open mouth. Our teeth collide, forcing us both to laugh hysterically. The mood becomes filled with perhaps a little bit too much levity, but that's okay, it's a nice change of pace. I kiss him again, tugging at his hair, burying my hands in his thick curls. When he pulls on mine, a shiver runs down my spine, filling me with an unusual sense of nervousness and desire all mixed into one.

If it's possible to lose ourselves in each other's arms, that's what has happened, and we're both better for it. His arms expertly make their way around my body and mine somewhat fumble around his. He takes the lead and I like that. He knows exactly how to make me feel good.

Our clothes come off piece by piece, slowly at first, but then faster and faster. Our naked bodies become entangled with each other. The hours that passed so slowly just before suddenly begin to move at warp speed. The sheets get wrinkled and the pillows fall to the floor. The headboard rocks as I grab onto it. Thankfully, because it's a rental in the middle of the woods rather than a motel room with walls, we don't bother dampening our voices, not even a little bit.

I extend the next morning as long as possible with coffee and breakfast in bed, putting as much of the case away from me as I can and keep it somewhere on the back-burner of my mind. There are more interviews to do, but I've convinced myself that it will be good to wait it out.

Really, I just want to spend more time with Dylan and put the rest of all of this out of my mind. It's well after one in the afternoon before I finally let the morning take hold. There are numerous calls from Gavin, who has not taken any time off and started early on.

"He's going to be really mad," I say, scrolling through the texts and missed calls.

"It's a good thing he's your subordinate." Dylan smiles, tilting his head.

He has his composition book out, writing in it in hieroglyphics with a thin, little mechanical pencil. It's open on his lap as he faces the patio and the looming forest outside. The bright blue sky and the sun are somewhere high above our heads.

"I'm going to go swim in the lake today," he announces. "Want to join me?"

I press my teeth close together and spread my mouth in an awkward smile, the kind that chimpanzees make when they're afraid.

"Don't worry about it." He waves his hand at me.

"Are you sure about that? Maybe I can go with you later."

"No, you've got to take care of this case. I'm fine on my own. I've got notes to write."

He shows me one half of a composition page that has been filled out. He hums the music for me, and I like the way it sounds.

"You're getting really good at this," I say.

"I've always wanted to learn to play music. I don't think I can be anything but a mediocre pianist, but composing, writing the symphony that's in my head, or at least trying to, has been the most exciting thing I've done in a while, besides dating you, of course."

I tilt my head and give him a little roll of my eyes.

"No, I'm serious," he says. "I love being with you, of course, but getting caught in that fire and the burns, it's kind of taken a toll."

Of course, I can only imagine.

"Just made me really evaluate what I want to do with my life, what I don't."

"And?" I ask.

"Well, it has just made me wonder what matters most besides you."

"I'm in the left side column on pros?"

"Definitely." He smiles. Grabbing my hand, he pulls me in closer for a kiss.

"But there's more to life than just work and relationships, right? There're hobbies, the things that I enjoy doing, and music has always been one of those."

"I know you've been taking some courses online."

"Definitely. I mean, just trying to find out what I can and can't do."

"Well, I'm really proud of you. I don't know if I say that enough, but I am. I mean, despite everything that has happened, here you are writing music."

"I wouldn't be here without you. You make it a lot easier."

He smiles and I kiss him again full of passion, love, and the kind of understanding that is difficult to describe. My phone goes off again and it's Gavin.

"I don't think you can ignore him all day. He's going to probably call 911 thinking something happened to you."

"He *is* 911." I smile. "Yes, I have to go talk to more of these teenagers. They seem to be clueless more than anything else."

"Weren't we clueless when we were teenagers?" He smiles.

"I mean, I certainly was. I spent all my time going to concerts, festivals, and anything to keep my mind off real life. I guess that's what being a kid is all about, pursuing all of those interests that you sometimes don't have time for as an adult."

When my phone rings again, I know that I have to answer it.

When I answer the phone, I can feel Gavin resisting the urge to lecture his superior about answering their calls. Instead, he just dives into the updates, which, unfortunately, despite his efforts aren't really that full of information.

GAVIN and I meet at the coffee place in town, Little Bear Coffee, a nice alternative to the chain stores, with fresh local coffee to boot. There's a large bulletin board in the corner with signs from local singer-songwriters and a job opening at the local used bookstore, which I find intriguing.

I stare at it for a few moments, trying to imagine what my life would be like if I could just give it all up, get this, become a used bookstore clerk and live life a little bit on my own terms. A little black cat comes over and wraps his body around my ankles. I kneel down and give him a pet. I see a painting of him in profile hanging prominently near the checkout and realize that this is Carly, the owner's cat.

Gavin and I meet up and talk about nothing in particular at first. He wants to get started right away, but I tell him to wait, ease into it more and actually take a little breather. I order him some coffee and a croissant. It seems to put him at ease, even if just for a moment.

"What were you doing this morning?" he asks. "I tried to call."

"Yes, I know," I cut him off. "I was busy."

He opens his mouth to ask for more details, but I glare at him and he shuts up. It's not his place. There's a hierarchy here after all and I don't owe him an explanation.

"Look, I know that you're here as a favor, but if you don't want to be, you don't have to be."

"Actually, that's completely untrue," I say. "I'm on vacation. My boyfriend nearly died, and this is our first time getting away. I was assigned to this case."

"We're all assigned," Gavin says.

"Look, I may not be doing my job up to your standards, but I'm not going to apologize for anything. There's hardly anyone working this case. I've done plenty of late nights and I needed a little break. That's what I did, that's what I took."

He lets out a deep sigh.

"If you don't want me working with you anymore, I can go right back home and not deal with it for a moment longer. You just tell me."

"No, I need your help," he says.

"Good. Because this girl is dead and one of her friends, or her boyfriend, or someone did this to her, either somebody at that camp or a passing drifter, right?"

I tilt my head. He shrugs.

"There are so many unknowns here, and a couple of hours of rest and relaxation is not going to change anything. You know that as well as I do."

He purses his lips.

"I speak from experience, Gavin. You need to take some time off, too. You can't let this consume you."

"I don't have a choice. There's no one else here."

"Yes, you do. That's exactly why you have to protect yourself. Remember on the airplane, you have to put your mask on first then your child's. You keep running like this, you're going to burn out. You're going to want to quit. That's exactly what happened to me."

I hadn't made plans to open up about this, but why not? He might as well hear about it. I want to stop him from making the same mistakes that I did. I tell him about the hours that I worked when I first started in LA, how eager I was to prove myself. I knew for certain that it was better for me to work there than the FBI, but at the same time, I wanted to rise quickly, I wanted to make the right friends. I wanted to do everything right. I outworked everybody.

I took on every bit of overtime and for what? It didn't matter in the end. I didn't make the right friends. I annoyed those around me. I annoyed the superiors.

Nobody likes an eager beaver. Nobody likes a know-it-all. No one likes to be outworked.

"Are you speaking about what I'm doing now, calling you on things that you don't want to hear?" Gavin asks, folding his arms across his chest.

"Maybe, but I'm also being a realist. I don't care. I'm going to give you a good recommendation because I think you're a good cop. Inexperienced, somewhat, but there's nothing you can do about that. Other people, they won't want to be showed up like that. You're going to run into them. There're plenty all over this department and others. They're going to see you as a threat and they're going to work with others to take you down. Not fire you or anything like that, but keep you a deputy forever, doing crap jobs, investigating nothing cases.

"This isn't television, Gavin. There's no reward for honesty and hard work. This is about playing the game the right way, but it's also about protecting yourself, treating yourself with respect, taking time off when you need it. That's what I did today. If you did interviews, you talked to people, I appreciate that. I want to hear all about it, but I also don't want you to make me feel bad for taking some personal time for myself, for having some work-home balance. I'm not burning out again, not for this job, not for this crappy pay, and neither should you, not if you want to have the long view of things, not if you want to do this until retirement."

He seems to take what I say to heart. I appreciate that because it doesn't come from a bad place, but from experience, and that's exactly how I mean it.

To refresh my mind, I open my notes about my conversation with Elizabeth and fill him in once again about what we spoke about.

"What are your thoughts about Elizabeth hiding her fight with Sarah?" I ask. "She didn't admit it until I really challenged her in the interview."

"There must've been a reason why she didn't want us to know," Gavin says. "Maybe because she was the one who wanted Dominic after all?"

"Yes, possible," I say. "She did tell me that if Sarah wanted him, she needed to make him wait and that she was angry at her for going to the room with him."

"Sarah told her about what happened in the motel room?" Gavin reviews the notes. "And Elizabeth didn't like it."

"Yes, that's what the fight was about." I nod. "Sarah accused her of being jealous, but she said that she was just looking out for her friend, which I don't exactly believe. She also insisted that if she had any interest in Dominic that he would be hers already. There were so many other things that I wanted to talk to her about, I admit, but the call from her mom cut it all short."

"What does this mean now?"

"Her mom told me to only discuss things with her lawyer from now on, that Elizabeth is underage and I have no right to talk to her."

"Is that true?" Gavin asks.

I nod. "Yes, especially if she's become a suspect. There's a fine line we're walking here because if she admits to something that she shouldn't, then it can be thrown out of court. Like, if she says was there and she did it. Depending on the judge, anything can be thrown out."

My thoughts return to Will and Erin and the case that will likely not see closure for a long, long time, if ever.

"What's the plan now? How involved do you think Elizabeth is?" Gavin asks.

I shrug my shoulders, take a sip of the coffee, and bite into the croissant that I absolutely don't want to eat, don't need to eat since I already ate a big breakfast with Dylan. The sugar hits me, lightening my mood, but not making my thoughts any clearer.

"I'm not sure if this is going to make a lot of sense," Gavin says, "but I found out a little bit more stuff by talking to the other campers."

"Yes? What?" I ask.

"Apparently, Elizabeth and Misty, Dominic's ex-girlfriend, had a falling out. They used to be close friends. When I talked to her about it, Misty said that Elizabeth was in an open relationship with a girl, another counselor by the name of Erica."

24

CHARLOTTE

The wind starts up again the way it has for hundreds of years, but instead of a breeze, it comes in gusts this time breaking through the everyday comforts of summer camp life. Erica Mercer tries to pull her hair up into a loose bun, but it just flies around her head in an unruly manner. The popsicle sticks and canisters of paints and little plastic cups filled with water are flying all over the place. I rush over to catch some of the items. Gavin does as well.

We get there too late, water splatters all over the place, but I collect the cups, stacking one on top of the other, and hand them to her.

"Thanks. What can you expect? I guess thunderstorms are rolling in."

She looks up and by the expression on her face, she seems like she is so much older than she really is. No crow's feet or lines, of course, she's sixteen, but there's a weirdness in her eyes. Her shoulders slope down, holding the weight of the world on them. I introduce myself to her. She shrugs her shoulders as if almost resigned to hear from me.

"You look like you were expecting me," I point out.

She shrugs again. She focuses on her art supplies. I don't know whether this is her avoiding me, or trying to get away from the tough questions, or just staying busy, waiting for the next group of campers to come around. One gust of wind follows another.

"What happens when you can't paint and do crafts out here?" I ask.

"It is what it is." She shrugs. "We try to make do."

"Does it rain?" I ask.

"Yes, sometimes." She nods. "Then we can go inside to the gym, but it's not the same."

"Do you like being outside?" She nods.

"No matter how hot it gets the trees, the sun, and the clouds, kind of give me inspiration. It's hard to explain."

"You're an artist."

"Yes. I teach art here and I have a YouTube channel."

"Wow, at your age?"

"Of course." She nods. "You have to start early if you want to get anywhere."

There's a seriousness to her tone. It's difficult to describe. It's like she's only a teenager, but she knows exactly what she wants in her life and what she expects from it, and nothing is going to stop her from getting it.

"Can you tell me more about yourself?"

"That's not why you're here, right?" she says as another gust of wind comes.

She holds the supplies close to her but then puts them down on the table, anyway. She places little rocks to keep the mats down and then she puts bigger ones inside the water cups so that they don't fly away this time.

"This should do," she says. "A lot of people don't like the wind, but I spent a few weeks up in Yucca Valley and the winds can get really bad out there."

"Yes, I know that place," I say. "You just get used to it. Sometimes in the summers, the flies come around as well; they're more bothersome, but you can just wear long sleeves and keep painting anyway, right?"

"I guess."

"I've never actually done art the way that you are doing it now."

"Then you're missing out."

"I don't think I'm very good at it," I admit.

"There is no, 'no good at art'." She shrugs. "You either make it or you don't, and then everything else is a matter of opinion, other people's opinions and you can't let them get into your head too much."

"I've never thought of it that way," I admit. I have spent so much time worrying about what other people would think of my writing that I've hardly managed to put any words down on the page. Gavin clears his throat and I remember why we're here in the first place.

"If you want to ask me any questions about Sarah," she says, "you should probably get to it."

She gives up trying to force her hair under a hair band and puts on a trucker hat, tucking everything underneath. She pulls off her oversized T-shirt and I see that she's average weight, wearing a sleeveless gray shirt underneath and overall shorts covered in paints.

"I wanted to ask you about Elizabeth."

She tilts her head, closing one eye, squinting in the sun. "What do you want to know about her?"

I can't tell if there's been a change of mood but something seems different when I bring up her name.

"I heard that you two were an item," I say as casually as possible.

She shrugs. "Yes, something like that."

"You weren't?"

"No, we were. We dated."

"Was she your first girlfriend?"

"Not at all."

"Do you identify as a lesbian."

"I don't identify as anything," Erica says. "I date who I want to date, and I don't discriminate based on gender or identity."

"Okay." I nod. "I understand. So, you've dated guys and girls?"

"Of course."

"What about Elizabeth?"

"Yes, she has. She likes both and some non-binary folks, too."

"What about you?"

"My pronouns are she and her," she says, looking me straight in the eye. I feel like this conversation is going a little bit off the rails.

"Can you describe the nature of your relationship?" I decide to go with a more open-ended question.

"With Elizabeth?"

I nod. She adjusts her cap. It's old and worn, well-loved, probably, with a stitched-on patch of a bear in the front and the name Quail Lake on the bottom, something purchased in one of the many gift shops in town.

"My relationship with Elizabeth was complicated," she says after a long pause.

"What do you mean by that?" I ask.

"I wanted to be exclusive. I know that's something that not many people want to do, especially in the kind of relationship that we were in, but I loved her. I just wanted to be with her, and I just wanted her to be with me. I made that perfectly clear, but she didn't feel the same way."

"So, did you break up?"

"No. She was fine with hooking up and after we had that conversation, I knew that she couldn't offer me any more than she already was. She liked guys too much or my opinion was that she wanted to be the kind of girl who was popular with guys. Maybe she wasn't ready to be exclusive with a girl yet, but it is what it is."

"So, how did you leave things?" I ask.

"Complicated. She came to talk to me one day and begged me not to break up with her when I said that I would. We talked about it for a while, and I finally caved. I'm not proud of it," she says.

On the horizon I see one of the first campers coming around. An eager girl with her hair in pigtails and a big smile on her face, someone who clearly is looking up to the cool experienced artist that Erica is.

"I don't want to talk about it around the little kids," she says. "It's not right."

"Okay. So, tell me now."

She waves hello to the camper and tells her to get started, that she'll be over in a bit. She pulls me aside and again, I'm in awe of this girl's confidence and experience, and her ability to compartmentalize where she is, where the other kids are, and her existence in the world from their perspective and the role that she plays in their life.

"I finally agreed to Elizabeth's terms, that we can keep things kind of secret."

"So, she wasn't ready to be out?"

"I wouldn't say that. People knew about us, but she wasn't ready to be exclusive."

"Do you think it was because it was you?"

"Yes, of course. I'm not exactly somebody who everyone is excited to be around. I mean, I state things as they are or as I see them and if you're being an ass I don't sugarcoat that and I don't put up with it. Elizabeth liked that until she didn't. She wanted the guys to be into her. She's that kind of girl, and maybe she'll change in the future but whatever. It was fine for the summer. I liked her enough and I wanted to be with her. I hate to admit it, but I was willing to do it on her terms."

"I see." I nod. "That's complicated."

"Yes. It is until it isn't. I met a girl in town. Told Elizabeth about it. She got mad but she couldn't do much about it, so--"

"How did you leave things?"

"We haven't. It's still up in the air. We fight a lot if that counts for anything."

"Okay. What do you know about her relationship with Sarah, her roommate?"

"Oh, Sarah was straight," Erica says.

"Yes, I know but any other interesting tidbits of information that you can offer me?"

More campers come in and sit down. Erica looks at her watch. I'm surprised to see that it's an Apple smartwatch rather than some old, preserved antique that she would have to keep winding. She looks at me looking at it.

"I like to count my steps." She calls me on it knowing exactly what I was thinking. "Don't put me in some category or slap a label on me and think that you know everything," she adds.

"Yes, I'm getting that sense." I nod. "Sorry about that."

She lets out a snort then folds her arms across her chest in defiance.

"Sarah?" I repeat the name to bring the conversation back to what I'm really here about.

"They were roommates, friends, and then not friends, they had some arguments."

"Anything else?"

"Something odd happened. I wasn't going to bring it up, but maybe it'll have some significance."

"Okay. Anything, of course."

"Elizabeth showed me Sarah's journal. The one that she had erased."

"What?" I ask.

"Yes."

"Can you explain that more?"

"She knew her password."

"It was her journal that she had on her Apple notes? Password protected, but Elizabeth knew the password?"

ERICA NODS. Then she doesn't say anything for a moment.

"What do you mean the one that she had erased?" I ask.

"I shouldn't have brought it up."

She hesitates and turns to walk away to talk to the campers, but I tug at her arm.

"Please. It may not be significant, but we want to find out what happened to Sarah, and any small clue could be a window into that."

"I don't think Elizabeth had anything to do with it."

"Okay, maybe not. I agree with you, but maybe there was something in that journal that could explain something; that's how these things line up and all come together finally."

"Okay." She takes a deep sigh.

"Sarah wrote a lot of things about Elizabeth in this journal on her phone. She had access to her iCloud account. Elizabeth had to use her computer once and Sarah told her the password. It was Dominic."

"The password?" I ask.

"Yes." She nods. "She liked him for a long time. I guess you're supposed to make the thing that you want your password so that you can manifest it. She believed in all that stuff. That's what it was, and then Elizabeth just brought that up. She looked up her iCloud account and she knew the password and she accessed her notes app and the journal."

"What was in the journal?"

"All these entries about how much she didn't like Elizabeth. Arguments they'd had, kind of mean stuff, but it was her journal. She was entitled to write whatever she wanted in it and Elizabeth should not have looked it up."

"So, she told you?"

"Yes. She told me that she'd read the journal and she told me that she'd erased the entries."

"Wow, that really took it to another level."

"That's what I thought," Erica says, glancing over at the picnic tables which are almost entirely filled with campers. "I've got to go. I told her that she was an ass for doing that and whatever. She got mad at me again. Told me that she should never have told me about it, blah, blah, blah. Elizabeth is a complicated person who likes attention, and I don't like that, but I like her. The other version of her that she keeps to herself and doesn't let anyone else see, but she's impulsive, which is probably why she deleted those entries. That's all I know. I've never seen them. Nothing else."

"Okay, I appreciate that. I might come back to follow up on some things later. Is that okay?" I hand her my card.

She shrugs. "Yes, do what you have to do."

Gavin and I exchange looks, and we know that we have to get CSI to look through Sarah's computer and any changes to her iCloud account as soon as possible.

25

CHARLOTTE

It doesn't take long for me to confirm with CSI that there were indeed changes made to the iCloud account, specifically the Notes app in Sarah's laptop. It does take a couple of hours for them to get back to me with the previous versions of those journal entries.

When they finally come back, Gavin and I meet up at the coffee shop from earlier in the day and go over the deleted entries. I read them myself, hand it over to him, and sip on my coffee, trying to process what I have read.

"Elizabeth deleted these," Gavin says after going through the entries.

I nod. I click my tongue and notice how dry my mouth is despite just downing an entire cup of black coffee.

"Elizabeth was threatened by these entries," Gavin announces.

As if I don't know, I take the phone out of his hand and read a few select lines.

I knew she would take him. I didn't want to tell her about my crush for a long time, but she somehow figured it out. Given how narcissistic she is, she's quite observant, and I guess she saw me looking over at him and everything that I said or didn't say, I never wanted her to know the truth. Anyone knowing about how I felt about Dominic would be like someone having naked pictures of me.

That seems pretty common nowadays, who hasn't seen naked pictures of their crush, but that would be me.

I never sent any to anyone and no one ever sent any to me. Elizabeth knowing how I feel about Dominic is my worst nightmare.

"She didn't want him to know anything." I sum up. "Elizabeth deleted these entries, and she didn't tell us that she knew anything about them."

"I guess the only person who knew was Erica," Gavin says. "She was probably not supposed to tell us."

"The question here," I say, thinking out loud, "is whether this has any significance, whatsoever."

"What do you mean?"

"This could just be some petty drama. Sarah didn't want Elizabeth to know about her crush on Dominic, roommate stuff, right? She didn't feel safe."

"In these later ones," Gavin interrupts. "She says that she's worried that Elizabeth would go after him just because she liked him."

"Yes, I guess that is the kind of girl that Elizabeth is, not exactly trustworthy."

"She seems like a terrible friend," Gavin says.

"Of course, I agree. The opposite of a friend really, but, of course, that doesn't mean that she had anything to do with her roommate's murder."

"Yes," Gavin agrees. "Like you said, this could have been all just some smoke and mirrors or a blip and an otherwise ridiculous friendship."

I press my lips together, thinking about what he has just said. I don't say anything for a few moments, uncertain as to how to feel about it.

Could it have significance? Of course. Elizabeth deleted the entries anyway, but didn't have to. Perhaps, she was spying on her friend, got upset about her saying these things about her, and then deleted the entries for no other reason than that she was impulsive, like Erica had said.

Gavin and I mull this over with a second round of coffee and croissants. I text Dylan that I'm running late once again, but this time, he says, "No worries," with a smile, and I feel a wave of relief rush over me. Hopefully, he's preoccupied with music, video games, or something else entertaining. It'll give me some space to work on this.

We go through the journal entries, rereading them over and over again, trying to get just a little bit more of a glimpse into who Sarah was as a person. All we can tell from this is that she was desperately in love with a boy who she wasn't sure wanted her back.

Unfortunately, the entries don't go as far forward as the motel room, no review of the day of her birthday and all the changes that had occurred in her life. That is, of course, assuming anything that happened that day had something to do with her murder in the first place.

Dominic is an easy scapegoat. Elizabeth, the terrible friend, is another. As far as actual evidence of one of them being involved in her murder, we don't have any. Not even close. What we have are a lot of rumors and speculation, feelings and obsessions that may or may not have anything to do with what had happened.

I check the dates just to make sure. The previous entries date back before her death. The last one, at least a week before.

"I still don't know exactly why Elizabeth deleted the entries," I say to Gavin. "I mean, why show her that she actually read them and exposed her snooping?"

Gavin nods his head, finishes the last of his chocolate croissant, and wipes his mouth with a napkin.

"Yes, I mean, I guess you could think of it that way," he says. "I got the sense that Elizabeth doesn't like to not get her way."

He slouches a little bit in his seat and folds his arms across his chest. I'm starting to see glimpses of the real Gavin Skeeter. A casualness appears, an easygoing spirit that he had hidden before behind a facade of eagerness.

I can't go so far as to say that he isn't entirely the eager, excited new guy-on-the-job personality that I had met earlier, but I'm starting to see another side to him. It's a side that I like.

"I knew a couple of girls like Elizabeth in high school, not exactly like her, of course. They have this air of I don't care. At the same time, they want everyone's attention and eyes on them. I don't want to stereotype. I'm painting with a wide brush.

"One of the reasons why she seems to not want to commit to Erica is that she would undoubtedly have the lesbian label on her. She could hook up, but she didn't want the guys in her life to think that she was off-limits. I wonder if it was the same with Dominic. He's this cool guy, friendly and popular that everyone likes, including her closest friend and roommate. She knows this but maybe she's wondering, 'What if I could get him interested in me?' It could be an ego boost, something purely narcissistic and completely self-involved.

"I don't think that she actually likes Dominic. I just think that she likes the power that she has over people. Her pretty face, her sexy body. She's on a power trip or perhaps might be on a power trip. I just wonder if when she read these journal entries that she saw just how desperate Sarah was for Dominic's attention, and how much she hated Elizabeth in that moment. Maybe she just lost it, deleted the entries, and just wanted to erase them from her mind. Since she couldn't do that, she erased some from the page."

Gavin is thoughtful and I can't help but agree.

26

CHARLOTTE

The day acquired a strange kind of haziness. It was particularly hot earlier and then the humidity blew in from God knows where, driving up the heat index. The mountains rarely get this way, but it is something that is all too familiar in the desert, especially in the summers. I get in my car, my hand pressed to the wheel, and drive nowhere in particular. Sometimes it's better this way. Get behind the wheel, lose yourself in what you're doing, and let the thoughts just roll over one after another.

My father called a few times, but I have yet to answer. I talk to Kelsey instead. We catch up, and I tell her that I still can't leave and can't make any plans to go to Seattle because there are things that I have to take care of here. I feel so close to finding out the truth. I'm on the precipice of something big, but what? I don't know exactly. Everything seemed to make more sense before, and now I'm just at a loss.

As I drive around the lake, I realize that it's not haze at all but a thick fog that has come over, probably from the mixture of cold air with hot and the impending thunderstorms that are going to bring their wrath down on the valley. The sun that had been filtering through the trees has all but disappeared, and the gusts of wind are getting stronger, shaking my car. Somewhere around the corner I see a sign for a thrift store, Great Lake Treasures. For some reason, I pull over and go inside. I have no reason to really be here, except that I need to clear my head. I've almost driven around the lake once. Sometimes it's good to just put your trust in whimsy.

The shop is musty and crowded, but the woman up front is friendly. Her head is buried in a book, and she only absently asks me about what's going on, if she can help me with anything, because we all know that you don't go to a thrift store with a goal in mind. That's what I like about them. You just never know what you're going to find and where it's going to lead you. Sometimes it's a bunch of junk. Let's be frank, most of the time it is. Then there are other times when you find an old book, rare, with a low printing. Not exactly valuable but something you might even want to read.

I was always fascinated with rare books and those mysterious rare book shops that never had any customers that would always exist in vacation spots. I was too intimidated to go in, but when I read about them online, I found out what exactly makes a book rare. It's when it has a small first printing, but then, for some reason, becomes popular or esteemed, and there are not enough books printed to satiate demand. Second and third printings are not the same thing as first. In the rare book world, first printing is what it's all about.

The thrift store doesn't have a huge book section, and the books that I do find are paperbacks of James Patterson and Danielle Steel novels, two of which I have already read and thoroughly enjoyed. I'd like to pretend to be someone who loves so-called highbrow fiction, but in truth, it leaves me a little bored and uninterested. There are only so many descriptions of the trees and the sky and how someone felt that I can take, when what I really want is a little bit of plot and character.

I WANDER around the thrift store looking at nothing in particular, touching everything. My hands get a thin layer of dirt on them. I keep going back to the books, reading the backs, thumbing through the pages, wondering if maybe one day one of my books will show up in a small thrift store in a lost mountain town in the hands of someone searching for answers.

Out in the back there's a big selection of children's clothes and toys, well-loved for a brief period and then given up for other children to enjoy. Dylan and I have not explicitly talked about having kids. Each time I've avoided the conversation, somewhat uncertain as to what I would even say.

I walk along the little aisles and a sense of claustrophobia starts to set in. The ceiling is not very tall, but as the clouds roll in outside the place gets darker and darker, until the clerk notices and flips on the lights. The aisles with the home goods are close together, with little tchotchkes all around.

Some are plastic, some are mysterious in their origin. Like, why would you ever donate a plastic cup that was meant for one-time use? Then why would you ever put it up for sale? Others seem worthy of the four dollar tag. I pick up a little glass jar, bright blue, and I look at the way the turquoise is reflected in the light, the color of the ocean. It looks like a fancy perfume bottle used up and then donated.

I pay with a credit card because I rarely carry cash. Just as I step out and get back in the car, across the street I spot Elizabeth standing, smoking a cigarette. Her head is buried in her phone. She's outside of a variety store that isn't exactly a thrift store, but more of a knickknack place. The sign out front says that there's even a soda fountain, like it's the 1950s.

Without giving it a second thought, I step into traffic and approach her.

"Hey there," I startle her. She pulls out her AirPods and looks at me, squinting her eyes.

"You're not supposed to talk to me."

"I'm not. I was just right over there, bought this little treasure," I hold up my glass bottle, "then I saw you. Aren't you supposed to be working?"

She shrugs.

"Are you even supposed to leave the camp? Listen, sometimes it gets to be too much, but you're a camp counselor."

"Yes, but that doesn't mean that I can't have time off."

She flips her hair.

"Do you have the day off?"

"No." She shakes her head. "What is the matter with you anyway? I'm not going to answer any more of your questions."

She's dressed differently, too. No Camp Quail Lake shirt, no oversized shorts. She's wearing makeup. This is a date.

"Are there a lot of counselors who sneak out of work when they're supposed to be there?"

"No. Only the smart ones do," she says with an air of superiority.

She shifts her weight from one foot to the other and I do the same. I'm very well aware of the fact that I shouldn't be talking to her, and that this conversation should be happening through a lawyer, but I can't help myself.

"You read Sarah's journal entries," I say, looking carefully at her expression. As soon as she hears the words, she looks up at me and squints. I'm onto something. She looks surprised. No matter how much she tries to recover, I know that I'm rattling her.

"How do you know about that?" She confirms what she had done.

"We found evidence. We found the deleted journal entries on her iCloud," I say. "We read the messages that you read. You didn't like them? You didn't like her writing about you? Is that why you deleted them?"

"I don't even know what you're talking about," she backtracks.

"I think you do," I say to put some pressure on. "What I'm wondering is why. Not why you read them. I mean, I know why, she's your roommate. You want to know what she's thinking, if there's a diary to read, that seems to be the thing to do when you're sixteen years old, but why would you delete them? She'd know that you read them for sure."

"Okay, so what?" she says.

"You're saying that you don't care, but then you wouldn't have deleted the journal entries if you didn't care."

"Haven't you ever done something impulsive?" Elizabeth asks, confirming almost everything Erica told me in that one line. "I was mad at her. I didn't want those words to exist. She had no right to write them."

"It was her diary," I say, "under a password."

"Yes, whatever. I mean, she must have known that I had access to them, right? I'm her roommate and I snoop, she knew that. She and I went through our other roommate's stuff."

"Who's?"

She bites her lower lip.

"None of that matters, okay?" she says, shaking her head. She goes into her crossbody bag, pulls out a cigarette, and then realizes that she's talking to a cop and that she's under eighteen.

"You're not going to tell anyone, are you?"

"I'm not here about you smoking a cigarette, though, I do think it's incredibly stupid."

"Whatever."

"You know how hard it is to quit those things? I mean, you might if you smoke them regularly, just terrible. Your breath smells, your skin smells, your hair smells. In a couple of years, it's not cool anymore, and no one wants to date a smoker."

"Whatever. Guys always want to date me."

"And girls?" I ask. Her eyes open wide.

"I have no problem with women being into women," I say.

"Well, you're not the only one in the world, are you?"

"What are you talking about?"

"Erica told you, didn't she? That's how you found out about the journal. We had this big fight," Elizabeth confirms the story for certain now. "Erica wants too much."

Elizabeth leans against the brick wall of the store, this time lighting the cigarette, inhaling, and sucking on it. I can see a little bit of the tension disappear in her face as the nicotine hits her system.

"Were you and Erica close?"

"Yes, of course. I love her and she knows that, but she wants the impossible."

"What does she want?"

"She wants me to just be with her." Her bra strap falls down and she doesn't pull it up to tuck it under her black tank top. Instead, she continues to suck on the cigarette and exhale just as feverishly.

"Erica and I were close. I loved her and she loved me, but she wanted more. She didn't want me to date guys. She didn't want me to be my whole self."

"Is that your whole self?" I ask. "You wanted to date other people? You didn't want to be exclusive?"

She bites her lower lip again and then turns to face me and I can see tears in her eyes.

"Of course, I wanted to be exclusive," she snaps. "I love her."

"What happened?" I ask. "Why aren't you together?"

"Because my parents would just freak out. I mean, they're not anti-gay people or anything like that, but me telling them that I have a girlfriend and that we were going to be together exclusively, they couldn't handle that. They were barely handling the rest of me, and they made all these threats about sending me away to some boarding school. I didn't want them to do that."

"Are you sure they were going to? They weren't just empty threats?"

"I was pushing my mom's buttons, and this was going to push her over the edge. I just knew that, for sure."

"Going back to the journal entries, why did you delete them?" I ask.

I stare at her and she breaks the tension by pulling out another cigarette as soon as she has put this one out.

"I don't want to hear it," she adds. "They help me relax."

"It would almost be better if you smoked marijuana," I say, and then immediately regret it. It's not the best for teenagers in terms of motivation and everything else, but there is mixed information about how addictive it is.

"What happened when Sarah found out?" I ask her.

"She got mad. What do you think happened?"

I get the strange feeling from Elizabeth that a part of her wants to tell me what is going on, and then another part is staying silent. I have to be careful and tread lightly about pushing her to the brink because if she had anything to do with Sarah's murder, any real involvement, all of that could be thrown out if her lawyer argued that I interviewed her without counsel or her parents presence. I don't know, of course, if she realizes the gravity of the situation. For now, I just try to push her buttons.

"She got angry that I got mad at her for how she was acting with Dominic. She thought that I was after him, and I wasn't really. I mean, he's cute and all, but I was just mad at her for how she was letting him treat her. She had waited so long, and then she just went to the motel room with him the minute that she could, the minute that he showed any interest.

"I wanted her to know that guys take that as something else. They may not know your history, but they think you're easy. I mean, it's a cliche, and it's so stupid, but if she wanted a serious thing with him, she shouldn't have done that."

"But your conversation with her didn't exactly come through like that, did it?"

She clenches her jaw.

"No, she thought I was jealous of her. She thought that I wanted to be with Dominic, and I let her think that."

"You know, Elizabeth, you're a smart girl, but you do stupid things."

"Please." She rolls her eyes.

"No, I'm serious. You want to be with Erica, but then you don't. You're afraid of your parents and what they would think when that's really what you want. You don't tell Sarah what you really mean and let her think that you want her boyfriend. You know, you're a threat, right?"

She smiles a little bit at the corner of her lips, and I realize that I had made a mistake. I shouldn't have said that. I shouldn't have given her the satisfaction, but I did.

"Listen, I have to go," she says abruptly. "I shouldn't be talking to you anyway; remember what my lawyer said? All of this has to be off the record."

"I'm not a journalist," I say. "That's not how it works."

"We'll see."

Suddenly, the armor is up and the Elizabeth that I had gotten to know earlier is back.

27

SARAH

I t wasn't that it was particularly good. Nothing had happened, but they had a moment. They'd shared something that was difficult to describe. They had held hands and he had kissed her and he had held her the way that she had imagined but also so much more real.

She thought there would be a soundtrack, music playing in the background, just the right lighting, but it was just the motel. Everything looked a little bit off. The fluorescent lights were a little too bright. The air conditioner blew a little bit too loudly. They had to talk over it, but when he pressed his lips toward hers the world fell away. When she pulled away the first thing she noticed was the musty smell of the curtains and the bedspread that was probably hardly ever washed, but she didn't care and neither did he. Then there was something else. They laughed. They laughed until they couldn't laugh anymore. She showed him funny videos and TikTok and YouTube and he showed her the memes that he had made for Reddit.

When she came home after the motel, right before dinner, Sarah felt like she had been existing in some parallel universe, much like our own but ever so different as well. The thing that pricked her bubble, that burst the balloon of this other world, she had walked in and found Elizabeth sitting on the top bunk, her arms crossed, staring at her with contempt.

"What did you do?" she snapped. "Why did you go there with him?"

At first, Sarah tried to deny being there but after a few moments she decided that there was no point. Elizabeth must have followed her or found out somehow. Plus, it's not like she really cared.

"I don't know how this is any of your business," Sarah said. "I was with him. So what?"

"You went to a motel with him. If you like him, you shouldn't do that."

"Oh, yes, that's coming from you, the chaste virgin?"

"I'm not saying that. I haven't always done the right thing. All I'm saying is that if you want him, you shouldn't do that. Dominic is not like you and the guys you date. They're all the same. Don't you get it?" Elizabeth said. "They're going to get tired of it."

"What you're trying to say is that he's going to get tired of me?" Sarah asked her.

She was mad at her roommate, but not for what she was saying, for the fact that she was here at all. She wanted her to leave. She wanted to be alone with her thoughts and relive what had just happened.

"This is, again, none of your business," she said after a long pause. "But nothing happened between me and Dominic."

"Yeah, right." Elizabeth rolled her eyes.

"I'm not going to try to prove anything to you since this has nothing to do with you. I don't even know why you're asking me anything," Sarah insisted.

She looked at herself in the dollar store mirror that she had brought from home, hating the warped image that it portrayed. It was hard to tell how her body actually looked. Was it like this or did the good mirror that she had back home reflect her real appearance? Did she only like that one because it made her look thinner? Or was this one the true reflection? There was no way to really know, and the whole thing seemed mildly like a scam. Regardless of how many times she told her to mind her own business Elizabeth wouldn't let up. There was something about the situation that had angered her, but Sarah couldn't care less. Not really. Then things got worse.

"You know that you don't have to be a slut, right? People will like you for who you are."

"Did you seriously just say that to me?"

Sarah turned around to face the girl that she had always considered a good friend. Certain words were off-limits. This was one of them. She wasn't drunk. She wasn't anything, and yet here was this word coming out of her friend's mouth. The one that had hurt her to the core of who she was. Something must have clicked in Elizabeth's mind as well because she looked a little flabbergasted when she had said it and immediately wanted to take it back, but for some reason she didn't. The bruise to the ego would be too much.

"You know what? I'm done talking to you," Sarah said, trying to take the upper hand.

She pulled her phone off of the charger, grabbed her bag, and started to walk away. When she got a few feet away from the cabin, she stopped dead in her tracks. She had turned to her journal to rant about what had happened, record her voice, get it transcribed, and keep it for later. She hadn't reviewed most of the entries, but she had named them appropriately, not often by the date, but by the topic, and the ones named Elizabeth, the one that she was going to add to, were all gone.

There were at least five other entries, about five different fights with her friend, except for this was going to be the first one. She scrolled up and down through her journal wondering if she had renamed them with the dates instead. Searched her name, but it was as if someone had deleted them all. Grabbing her phone, Sarah rushed back into the cabin, catching Elizabeth in the bathroom with her underwear around her ankles.

"Do you mind?" Elizabeth snapped.

"Yes, I do mind," she said, without closing the door.

"What's this?" She pointed her phone at her friend.

"I have no idea."

Elizabeth tried to act like she didn't care that she'd gotten interrupted while going to the bathroom. She got up, pulled her shorts up, and went to wash her hands in the sink.

"What's this?"

Sarah came over, bringing the phone so close to Elizabeth's face that she could feel the heat from it radiating into her skin.

"I have no idea what you're talking about," Elizabeth said.

Sarah insisted, "What happened to my journal entries?"

Elizabeth shrugged.

"You deleted them? You went through my phone, and you saw that I wrote in my private diary some crap about you and you just deleted them?"

Elizabeth shrugged.

"How could you do that?"

"How could I do that?" Elizabeth asked. Her face got red and flushed. "How could you even ask me that? How dare you write all that crap about me and rant and rave about whatever?"

"In my private journal?" Sarah corrected her. "I didn't do it publicly, I didn't do it on social media."

"It doesn't matter."

"How long have you been reading my journal?"

"I just happened upon it."

"No, I don't think so." Sarah narrowed her eyes. "I don't think you just happened upon it. I think you've been doing it for a while. I wonder how many other entries are missing of things you didn't like."

"You had no right to write about me. I don't want you to have my name in your mouth."

"You know what? This is a free country, and I can do whatever I want."

Elizabeth tried to get past her. Their shoulders touched ever so slightly, and this was the trigger point. Sarah pulled her hair back and Elizabeth fell.

Elizabeth yelled, "Ouch!" and slapped her with an open hand. Sarah jumped on her, made a fist, and punched her in the face. They continued to fight and tussle with one another, hair flying, hands cramping, fingers getting pinched.

28

SARAH

I t took a while for her to recover from the physical altercation. She'd never been in a fight before, not even close, and having that kind of bodily contact with someone felt insane. I mean, she'd never even had sex with anyone and here she was in the most physical fight she'd ever been in. A lot of kids fight when they're little, but Sarah had never been in one and actually, neither had Elizabeth. The altercation changed them, not for the better.

Sarah couldn't imagine sleeping in the same room with her and yet, she knew that she didn't want to report this to Dr. Abbott or anyone else out of fear of getting in trouble. There was a zero tolerance policy when it came to physical acts of violence and they would both be told to leave if anyone found out.

They fought alone, no one caught them and when they pulled away, they both sat at opposing sides of the room, nursing their wounds like hurt animals. Neither of them said a word, but what was unspoken was that they would not come forward and confront one another or tell a soul.

At least, this was what Sarah had hoped would happen and had promised to herself. Nevertheless, after she had covered up some of the bruising on her face with makeup and with a thick layer of foundation, a baseball cap, and an oversized sweatshirt, she left with a small bag. She rode her bike to town, not wanting anyone to see her. It was getting late, past dinnertime, and she knew that her friends would be calling to see where she was. She waited for a while, but no one called. It occurred to her that Elizabeth had probably made an excuse for her, for both of them, if she had indeed stayed in the room. No one else called her phone either, including Dr. Abbott or any of the senior counselors, so she doubted that Elizabeth had come forward about their fight.

Sarah wandered around aimlessly. She wasn't hungry and all the shops were closed. She found herself on the outskirts of town in the one movie house playing Stephen King's *It*, the old one. It had occurred to her that she had never seen it. Maybe a little bit of horror would put the day in perspective. It had been quite a roller coaster. Something that she wasn't exactly used to. She was one of the few people in the theater. She sat in the back in a cheap uncomfortable faux-leather chair, nothing like the new theaters that she had been to all her life. There was no reclining. There was hardly even any padding.

As the movie started, she let it roll over her. She tried not to pay attention. She tried to get into the story and to not let the fact that it was old and everything about it that reminded her of the '80s, or was it the '70s? Whenever it came out. She tried not to think about that and instead focused on the story, but she couldn't. She kept getting distracted. She kept checking her phone for messages from her friends or Dominic or anything. Then when the horror started, she was finally able to pull away and immerse herself in the movie.

Sometime later when the wind started up again outside, Sarah decided to leave. The movie wasn't over yet, but she couldn't focus anymore. The images in the story weren't enough to pull her in.

It was nothing about the movie itself, it was that her thoughts were occupied elsewhere. She wasn't sure if she could return to camp, and she now regretted leaving in the first place. She shouldn't have. The cabin was as much hers as Elizabeth's. Now

Elizabeth would probably turn their friends on her. Her story would be the first one heard, the first memorialized. She of all people knew how important it was to get to the friends first. Nevertheless, she couldn't go back to her room, and she knew she couldn't sleep there.

For some reason, when she came out of the theater, she saw the clerk putting butter all over the popcorn, popping fresh kernels without bothering to clean out the rest. She knew that the theater was old and in need of some tender loving care because the M&Ms that she had just consumed tasted stale and the paper bag itself was a bit weathered. Maybe they were as old as the movie that she had seen. By the bathrooms right to one side near Ms.. Pacman, the original arcade game, she saw a payphone with scratches and notches on the side. She had never used one before but had seen it on television. She had a few quarters in her wallet. She had no idea how much it cost, but she put in seventy-five cents and dialed Dominic's number from her phone. There was no particular rhyme or reason for this, except that she just wondered if he would pick up a strange number. Unlike her, he did.

"Hello?" he asked, his voice sounded confused on the other end.

"It's me," she said, hoping that he would recognize her voice, but knowing that he probably wouldn't.

"Sarah, why are you calling me on this number? Did you lose your phone?" he asked without missing a beat, and a big smile came over her face. So the day was not imagined. He had actually liked her, and he actually wanted to spend time with her. Then all of a sudden, without much consent on her part, tears started to run down her cheeks. He called her name again, and instead of talking, she let out a big whelp.

"Are you okay?" he asked.

She shook her head.

"No," she finally managed to say a word. "I'm sorry. I don't mean to cry. It's just that something happened with my roommate. It's so stupid," she mumbled through the words. "It is my birthday and I want to celebrate, but I just--"

"Let's meet up," he interrupted her right away. "I want to see you. Why didn't you tell me it was your birthday?"

"I don't know." She shook her head as if he could see her through the phone. Nothing she was doing right now made much sense. Not to her, not to him, but she didn't care. She just wanted to see him, kiss him, have someone tell her that it was going to be all right.

Sarah waited for him outside of the Wagon Wheel Motel, sitting in the parking lot on her bike, biting her nails. She had twirled her hair so much that it curled at the ends and had moved on to another nervous tic that had popped up whenever she felt stressed. The butterflies in the pit of her stomach were different this time.

There was an element of excitement to it, just like earlier in the afternoon. Somehow, everything that had happened with Elizabeth almost didn't matter, because she was going to see Dominic again.

She saw him in the distance riding his bike, the reflectors shining the way. They were not supposed to leave the campground, and they would both be in trouble if anyone found out. This was particularly bad at night given the fact that the roads were winding and they had nothing but their bikes. It had started to drizzle, but not so much that the weather had bothered her, but her shirt had gotten a little damp and her hair got a little bit curly from the humidity that had suddenly sparked up.

"What happened to your face?" Dominic asked as soon as he pulled up.

She had forgotten that foundation can be removed with a little bit of water, and she had rubbed both her tears and the rain off her face.

She pulled up her hood over her head and turned away from him.

"Nothing," she snapped.

Sarah was angry with him. She furrowed her brow and started to walk away, but he held onto her arm, holding her closer.

"Let go," she said.

"Do you want me to leave?"

The question caught her by surprise. It was so direct on the nose and yet she couldn't say no. Instead, she glared at him, their eyes locked on one another's.

He grabbed her hand and she realized that he wasn't just trying to hold on to her. He had taken the lock that she had yet to put on her bike to secure it to the post out of her hand. When she let go, he did it for her. These little moments of helpfulness were not something that she was used to, not at all. It made her feel conflicted about him. He just did these kinds of things without asking her permission, and it felt something like a father or a brother would do, but in a good way, to help out. Nevertheless, she was still mad at him for calling out her bruises, the ones that she'd tried so desperately to hide. Couldn't he tell that she was embarrassed, that she didn't want anyone to know?

They went to the motel room to which they still had access, having paid for the night. He kissed her on the threshold before they even got the key in the hole. She kissed him back, turning into his arms.

When they kicked off their shoes, the carpet felt squeaky underneath her bare feet. It had an odd rubbery texture, as she pushed off and brought her lips closer to his. He cradled her head in his hands, burying his fingers in her hair and tugging ever so slightly. Her hands found their way under his shirt and pulled it over the top of his head. This time they didn't laugh. This time they just felt around for one another in the dark, not bothering with the lights.

"WHEN ARE you going to tell me about the bruises?" Dominic asked afterward when they lay in bed, tangled up in the sheets.

Sarah bit her lower lip, but appreciated him asking anyway. It showed that he cared. She liked the way that he called her on her lies. It was refreshing. There was an honesty there that she never thought that she would have with a guy.

"I got in a fight with Elizabeth. She deleted my journal entries, the ones about her."

"She read them?"

"Yes," Sarah said. "She went in there and just deleted them all. I couldn't even believe it."

"Did she have your password?"

"I guess I gave it to her at one point a while ago when she had to use my computer, but I never thought that she would actually go through my notes and go through everything. I was so pissed."

"You have every right to be, of course. How did all those marks happen?"

"We started arguing, then we started fighting. She put her hands on me. I punched her and we scratched each other's faces. When it was happening, I thought someone would break it up, but no one came. After a while, we just got tired."

"You can get kicked out for that. You know that."

Sarah nodded.

"That's why I hope you don't tell anyone. I'm sure Elizabeth won't either. Do you think they'd kick both of us out?" Sarah asked after a moment.

He nodded.

"I remember the fight last year. That kid was getting bullied and picked on all the time. He finally fought back, but they kicked both of them out. You're not supposed to put your hands on anyone. It wouldn't be a safe environment otherwise."

"Yes, but getting made fun of and told you're nothing but scum. That's totally fine with the camp. Right?"

Dominic exhaled deeply. In reality, there wasn't that much bullying going on at camp. They were counselors and they were keeping the younger kids in line.

"Elizabeth and I never fought like that before, so rough. We had some arguments, but this was different."

"You're worried that she might go to Dr. Abbott and make something up?"

"No, not really," she said. "There are bruises and scratches on both of us so she should be getting kicked out as well. I think we're going to handle this privately."

"Do you want me to say anything?"

"No. Please don't. This whole thing was partly because of you."

"Because of me?" He sat up in the bed and leaned against the back with a wry smile starting to stretch across his face.

"Don't get so cocky." Sarah laughed.

"Well, I've never had two girls fight over me before. It's cool."

"Please, she just got all mad at me for going to the motel room with you earlier. It was so out of the blue. Why does she even care?"

"What did she say exactly?" Dominic asked.

"She just said that I shouldn't act like that, that you'd take advantage of me."

"Little does she know that you wanted everything that you got."

"Oh, please. Don't be such a dick," Sarah said, and they both laughed.

"Why? Do you think she has a crush on me?"

"I have no idea. She just got so mad at me for going to the motel and said that you wouldn't treat me the same afterward. Said that you would just use me. I don't know, whatever. I'm tired of talking about her and all of her crap."

"Okay. What do you want to talk about instead?"

She smiled and gave him a wink. He leaned over and kissed her.

29

CHARLOTTE

I get a call from Nick at the Wagon Wheel Motel just as I sit down for some Pad Thai with Dylan.

"I have to take this," I say, looking at the number, but not bothering to get up from the table.

Dylan gives me a casual shrug. He's used to it by now. He pulls out his own phone and pops in his AirPods to listen to a podcast.

"She was here," Nick says. "She was here in the afternoon and then she came back later. I just found the footage."

"Later that night?" I ask.

"Yes."

As soon as I hang up the phone I stare at Dylan as he takes a bite. When he asks me what's wrong, I tell him about Sarah being at the motel with Dominic. He asks me more but that's all I know.

"Would you mind coming with me to talk to the clerk after dinner?"

"Are you sure you want to even have dinner?"

I nod, knowing that I've been neglecting him way too much. I try to think of something else to say and nod along when he suggests a topic of conversation, but nothing clicks. After a while he gives up and asks me more about the case.

"Listen, I'm sorry about all of this, again," I say, finally shaking my feeling of detachment and being lost in the zone. "I don't mean to have this case occupy so much of my life and our trip."

"Don't worry about it," he says, tossing his hair a little bit out of his face. "I gave up on you on this trip and I figured I'd enjoy myself, nevertheless. It's a nice town."

"I'm surprised you wanted to come here or had agreed, given the accident," I say, taking a sip of my water. This is the first time that I had brought that up. The accident wasn't too long ago, and the scars on his body are still healing. I don't know if the ones in his mind ever will. He gives me a shrug.

"I've had worse things happen. It's no big deal, really."

"Your partner dying?"

"Folger wasn't a close friend. I've lost a close friend before and that hurt like hell. This was just a guy that shouldn't have done so many drugs before going to work that day. If anything, I'm pissed at him. I wonder if he'd be dead and I'd have all these burns if he actually wasn't some degenerate in the first place."

I give him a slight nod, feeling slightly uncomfortable by the sudden heat in his tone.

"Sorry," he corrects himself. "I mean, I know it's an addiction, it's a disease, all that stuff, but now that you brought it up, yes, I guess I am pissed off at him. But being here at this lake, it's pretty, I like the pine trees, I like that it's not 115 degrees outside. What's there to complain about?"

"Me agreeing to spend a week on vacation with you and then leaving you high and dry to work on the case," I point out.

"All that means is that you owe me."

"I owe you?" I ask.

"Yes. An apology, a debt, a favor, however you want to think about it." He gives me a wink. "You have to make it up to me."

"I will." I lean over the table and give him a big kiss. He kisses me back, slipping me the tongue just a little bit and I laugh.

30

CHARLOTTE

We get to the Wagon Wheel Motel where the scent of musty humidity overpowers me in the lobby. It had recently rained and Nick, the clerk, is dealing with an overflow. There's a hole in the roof and he is setting up pots and pans to catch the water.

"Sorry about this. I keep telling them that I need to get this roof fixed. I swear it rains and snows in here all the time and it just—they don't care."

"It's not that I don't care," Carson comes in. "It's that I'm barely breaking even on this place and replacing the roof on an old building like this is going to cost a pretty penny."

He gives me a nod. We've met before, talked a bit, and he knows exactly why I'm here. I like the banter between him and the 18-year-old, so friendly, like equals when they're anything but.

"This is my nephew, Nick," Carson says. "He's got a smart mouth, and he's staying with me for the summer because his mom kicked him out." Even though he's complaining, he says it in a very proud and loving sort of way.

"Hey, I don't have to be here if you don't want me to," Nick says, putting his hands up, "Looking through all this footage for the cops, I was the one that found it you know."

"Good," I say. "I appreciate that."

Dylan smiles, leaning slightly, looking through the pamphlets near the front door.

"There's paragliding here?" he asks, breaking the tension.

"You're here because I don't want you to be at the bus station, asking people for change." Carson laughs and then embraces his nephew in a warm hug.

They show us the footage and I clearly see Dominic and Sarah going back to their room later that night.

"How did we miss this before?" I ask, using the non-accusatory 'we' when it was really just them.

"I had no idea that they came back. I just happened to find it when I was scrolling through the rest of the day since they did pay for the whole time, but they left and took their bags. The place was basically empty," Nick says.

"I appreciate you getting this. This is huge. How long did they stay?"

He scrolls through, and it's over two hours. "Any idea where they went after?" Nick asks.

"No. They were on their bikes. You can see them taking them and heading back."

"I'm assuming back to the camp, right?"

"Yes, I guess so," I say. I don't mention the fact that she had just gotten into a physical fight with her roommate and perhaps going back to camp was out of the question. "But they definitely left?" I ask.

"They left the motel room. I can scroll through and try to find out whether they ever came back again, a third time."

"It's a possibility," I say. "Maybe they went to get some food."

He scrolls through for about an hour, but we don't see anything.

"Would you mind going through the rest of the footage?" I ask. "If it's not too much trouble."

Of course, I'm going to send this over to CSI, but it's going to take them a lot longer to get back to me than this teenager.

"Of course." He nods.

Dylan and I walk out after I take video of the footage at the motel with my phone.

"He lied again," I say. "How long am I going to keep falling for it? Do you think he did it?"

"I don't know, but I have no idea why he's keeping all of this secret either. It's just ridiculous."

I pace back and forth outside of the motel, tapping my fingernails on my leg.

"All these layers of this onion are just getting to me," I say. "Going back and forth, interview over interview, them admitting a little bit."

"But isn't that like your job?" Dylan asks, and I laugh.

"Haha, very funny."

"Well, not every case can be so simple to solve, right? They have to make it hard for you."

I just wish that we could get some of this DNA evidence back quickly. I mean, that would tell us a lot. On the other hand, they're all underage. It's going to be very complicated to get them. You have to deal with all these lawyers and parents. Every time I talk to those kids, I'm just worried that they're going to say too much and it'll get thrown out of court. I guess I'm a little bit traumatized by what happened to Will.

"Well, he actually had a relationship with the primary suspect, so that's a little bit different."

I roll my eyes.

31

CHARLOTTE

The bugs are going nuts tonight as I stand outside of Dominic's cabin trying to piece everything together. The lies that these kids have spun have made my head swirl and yet it is in these lies that I will find the truth, and justice for Sarah. I had called for the autopsy results, but they're still yet to come in, as well as the DNA and so, for now, the truth lay in what they would have said, or could have said, and the pieces of the truth that would come out together through the lies.

As far as primary suspects go, Dominic is at the top of the list. There is still the possibility that there was an intruder, a stranger, in the camp, but the likelihood of that is small and now it would have to be something that would be confirmed if the DNA came back and didn't match any of the suspects here.

Dominic's friends could have also participated, covered it up. I already knew that they had covered up for him before, and I have yet to figure out who was the last person to have seen her alive.

The birds chirp unusually loud above my head, adding their voices to the night bugs. Dylan is waiting for me a little bit down the path, away from the cabin, giving me space to do my job.

"This is the first time that I have seen you like this in the middle of your interview and everything else," he says when I give him a slight nod. He urges me to head back toward the car, but I shake my head no. Instead, I just put one foot in front of the other and we make our way around the camp and then onto the trails out back. These are the same trails that Sarah and Dominic had taken to get to town. I look around at the trees to see if there are any cameras anywhere but that's too much to hope for. There's that old question. If it's not recorded, did it ever even happen? The answer is, of course.

Just because you don't know that something had occurred doesn't make it not true. Positioning yourself or the camera and the footage that you would've watched at the center of it is positioning yourself in the center of the universe and that's just not the case. If anything, you're an observer. You're standing before a river watching it pass by choosing to step in at one point or another knowing that you can never step into the same river twice.

"What are you thinking?" Dylan asks.

I turn to face him. I take his hand in mine.

"I'm glad you're here. This would be a lot harder to do without you," I say.

"You're an expert. You would've handled it."

"Yes, maybe, but each case takes a toll, you know. Kind of wears on you, and after a little while you end up wondering how many more of these cases you can take. Missing girls, dead young women with their whole lives before them. She was just living her life. She did nothing wrong. She didn't deserve this."

He looks at me, narrowing his eyes. I had said something. I had said a *faux pas*.

"Don't look at me like that," I add "You know what I mean."

"No, not exactly. Are you saying that if she was a prostitute on the streets then it wouldn't be as sad?"

"Of course, it would be sad but I'm only human. This girl had a whole future ahead of her. She was going to go to college. She was going to do something great, and some asshole decided to take that away from her."

He tilts his head. He's trying to make me go there. He's trying to get me to admit that if she were a crack addict on the street I wouldn't feel as bad. It's not exactly true. If I got to know that crack addict, knew her struggles, why she was leading the life that she was leading, what led her there, and all the terrible people that were involved in those decisions that she had made, then of course I'd care the same way.

"I just see this girl as a young me, you know," I say after a long pause. "If your life had ended when you were her age, how much would you have missed out on? How much growth, challenges, all that stuff? How much happiness, how much sadness? Back in LA, I investigated every case that came across my desk with the same ferocity. The crack addict and the nice girl. Who never snuck out, who never even smoked pot, and it wore on me because most of the time you don't get the answers you're seeking. How many murders and missing persons are found out there? You know as well as I do that it's hardly any."

"This one we have a shot at. Do you think that it--?" Dylan asks.

"I hate to say but it's probably Dominic. He has lied to me so much. His story keeps changing. He's acting like he's covering up for her, but I think he might be covering up for himself."

"What about pressuring his friends, trying to double-check his story?"

"Yes, that's what I'm going to have to do. There are so many things that aren't adding up. This is really the direction to go."

We walk hand-in-hand down a dusty path surrounded by towering pines which look menacing in the dark. There's nothing but moonlight illuminating our way and the chirping birds and the buzzing bugs somehow make it feel even more solitary. When I step on a twig, it makes a loud cracking sound as it snaps under my foot. A couple of miles down the road the path ends, and I see the 7-Eleven and the motel perched slightly on the side of the hill.

"This is why they went here," I tell Dylan. "The shortcut to the trees is pretty and cuts off a good chunk of the road. I didn't realize it didn't take them that long to get here. We should probably head back and get our car. Let me pop in again and confirm the story."

"What do you think?" Dylan asks as we walk up to the motel. "Do you think he's telling the truth, that they stayed there until 5:00 a.m.?"

"No," I say as my first gut visceral reaction, but then I change my mind. "Well, actually, maybe. It depends on when she was killed. I don't think that he held onto her body for very long."

We walk into the all too familiar lobby, the one I feel like I've been in one hundred times today. The musty smell immediately settles in the inside of my nose but this time it's punctuated by a little bit of bleach. Someone had clearly cleaned something right before we arrived.

"You're back," Nick says.

"Yes, I have one more question for you." He nods. "The guy that Sarah was with is insisting that they stayed until five in the morning. They didn't leave the room until then. Any chance you can confirm or deny that?"

"Yes, we can take a look. Shall I look around five?"

"Yes." I nod. "I mean, that's what he said. If we don't find it, then we can expand the search but let's do that for now."

What I don't tell Nick is that I had challenged Dominic on this. I told him that I didn't see any video of it, and he said that he had left another way. We look through the lobby and the two cameras set up in the parking lot, eventually finding the fact that he did leave the motel at 5:10.

Only, he was alone. Four minutes later, however, there's footage of Sarah leaving her room alive and well but going the opposite direction from Dominic, headed north on Lake Road. Dylan and I stare at the footage, and I can't help but shake my head.

"Why wouldn't he tell me all of this right from the beginning? What is he hiding?" I snap at Dylan. "I mean, why do I have to pull all of this information out of him bit by bit, come here to confirm everything? It's ridiculous. He has his alibi, he went to the motel and came back again. They stayed here all day. That's the last time he saw her. Why doesn't he want me to know that? Why is he covering and for whom?"

"Definitely not for himself," Dylan adds.

I give him a nod. I mean, it's possible, but why?

It's like none of this makes any sense. I pace back and forth in the motel asking to see more footage. I watch her walk away and disappear.

I zoom in on the parking lot to check the other cars that are there. Only some of the license plates are visible and I write them down. I have no idea if this means anything, but I have very little to go on at this point except for Dominic's torrent of lies.

Then suddenly, in the corner of the parking lot by one of the street lights I spot a bicycle. We zoom in a little bit but the footage is still grainy, but I recognize it anyway. There's a basket in the front with a little flower attached to it and I remember exactly where I had seen it before.

32

CHARLOTTE

"What is it?" Dylan asks as I peer into the camera, staring at the bike that's locked to the light post. It's a beachcomber with thick, wide wheels and a shiny turquoise body, which of course, I can't see since the footage is black and white. There's a large metal basket attached to the front and an oversized plastic Daisy flower is attached to the metal rungs of the basket for no other reason but decoration. I can see the flower in my mind's eye, yellow on the outside with big white petals all around. Though it looks small, insignificant, here in the frozen footage before me, I know exactly who that bike belongs to because I had seen it outside of her cabin.

"This is Bennett's bike," I say, pointing to the screen. "Sarah's roommate. What is it doing here?"

Dylan looks at me. "Are you sure?"

"Yes."

"How do you know?"

"I saw it outside the cabin. I saw her riding it and mostly because I always wanted a bike like this as a kid and it just drew my attention."

"You wanted a beachcomber with a basket?" He laughs.

"Yeah, and even this flower. It's exactly what I would have done. It was also odd because Bennett didn't seem like the type of girl who would have something like this."

"Are you sure that it's not one of the other roommates?"

"I saw her riding it a couple of times, so probably not."

"But what does she have to do with this case?" Dylan asks.

"I have no idea." I shake my head. "She's the last person I thought would even be here."

When we get back to our own cabin, I call Gavin to fill him in on what we found and brainstorm the best way to approach talking to her. In the middle of the night, pulling her out of bed would definitely put the most pressure on her, but whether it would get us the answers that we want, I'm not so sure. I feel like the middle-of-the-night conversations should be reserved for ones that are definitely going to lead to arrests. And in this case, whatever evidence I have, actually points to someone else entirely.

"No, we need to talk to Bennett when she's comfortable, at ease, has nothing to suspect," I say to Gavin on the phone. "Sometime tomorrow morning, I'll check her schedule with Dr. Abbott. I don't want to pull her away at breakfast and create a firestorm of rumors or anything like that. I think the best way to handle this is with as much tact as possible. Kid gloves and all that."

Gavin agrees with me mostly because I sound certain and set in my ways, but I wonder if he actually agrees with me.

When you present yourself and your opinion in a certain way, people just go along with it. It's hard to question authority. I wonder if that is the best way to approach Bennett. I need to gauge her reaction. Will she be shocked to be found out that she was there? Will she deny it right away or will she jump around a little bit, act surprised?

People act like you can tell so much from people's reactions and body language, but the truth is that people react the way they're conditioned to react. A person living on the street, fighting for their life on a daily basis will have a completely different set of reactions to questions from someone living a comfortable life who has never had to be really challenged or questioned before. Either way, we need some answers and whatever answers that she's willing to provide will be much appreciated.

I toss and turn most of the night. It gets so bad that at one point I see that I keep waking up Dylan and feel bad and head to the living room to the couch. This is the first time that we've slept apart in the time that we've been together and weren't sleeping over and it feels oddly strange, like a little bit too familiar in a married old couple kind of way.

Nevertheless, I turn on the TV, let the blue glow wash over me, and just flip through the channels, lying on one side, my other arm buried underneath my pillow. Dawn can't come quick enough, but it is only when the sun starts to peek in through the windows, just a little bit, that I start to feel sleepy and let myself drift off and get a few hours of deep sleep.

When I wake up, I see that it's well past nine a.m., and jumping out of bed, I accuse Dylan of letting me sleep too much.

"You didn't sleep at all," he says. "I turned down your phone. This can wait. You need your rest." With that, I know that I have a keeper in my life.

GAVIN MEETS me outside and we head over to Bennett's cabin. The bikes are there right by the side, locked up next to the cabin, and one of them is a perfect match to the one I saw on the video camera.

"That's it," I say, pointing to Gavin.

I pull out my phone and show him a screenshot. Even though it's black and white and the bright turquoise color of the body of the beachcomber is not visible, and neither is the little yellow interior of the daisy on the bike itself, it's a perfect match.

"Unless there are others that are exactly like this," I say, "chances are it's Bennett's."

"But how do you know it's actually hers? There're like three other bikes here."

"We'll ask one of the roommates, anyone else at camp. Come on, you know how it is, Gavin. Everyone knows what you drive."

"What do you think is the significance of all this?" Gavin asks, shifting his weight from one foot to the other.

It's mid-morning and he looks like he had a good night's sleep. Bright-eyed and bushy-tailed is his go-to look, but I like that about him. Cynicism can be entertaining, but it gets boring after a while, it's also hard to keep going with that mindset. You need someone eager, someone willing to take chances, to work harder, and cynicism is like a damp blanket that lays over you, suffocating you slowly from the outside in.

"Hey, what are you doing here?"

Bennett pops up behind us. She catches me by surprise, but I try not to show it.

"We were actually just going to try to find you," I say.

"Yeah, I had fifteen minutes between my sessions, and I forgot to charge my phone last night."

She walks past us, opens the door, walks inside, plugs in her phone, and then pops back out in the doorway.

"So, what did you want to talk to me about?" Bennett asks, putting her hand over her brow, blocking the sun. She has nice skin and bright inquisitive eyes. She's smiling from ear to ear, and I can't tell if this is a façade.

The shadows of mid-morning are getting shorter and shorter. The tall pine trees don't provide much shade, but still enough for a little bit of shelter. The morning is unusually warm. Most days it hovers in the high sixties, but this time it's almost eighty and it's going to be a hot one.

I run over all the different ways that this can go in my head.

Do I add a lot of pressure and force her to admit something on the spot or do I take it slow and hope something will slip out? There's only one way to go. You only get one chance and if anything, it relies on your gut.

"Is that your bike over there?" I ask, trying to get her to confirm which one of the bikes is hers first and foremost. She seems surprised by that question. She looks down at her sneakers and then back at me, puzzled.

"Do you mean the ones out back?" Bennett asks.

I nod.

"Yes, those are all of our bikes."

"Do you use yours to get around?"

"Well, there have been some instances of theft and there isn't a place to lock them up everywhere. I usually walk since everything's pretty close."

"Uh-huh," I mumble. "Which one of the bikes is yours?"

"Oh, the prettiest one of all." She smiles proudly. "The turquoise with the flower."

A small smile forms at the edge of my lips. It is her bike after all.

"In what instances would you say that you use your bike?"

"To go to town, run some errands, mainly to leave the camp. Why? Did something happen to it?" Bennett goes around the patio and looks back, satisfying her curiosity that the bike is intact. She walks back toward me. "God, you scared me. I thought it was in an accident or something."

"How would it be in an accident that you wouldn't know about?"

"I don't know." She shrugs. "Maybe some car backed into it."

There's a long pause. I tilt my head slightly in her direction and she looks at me.

"Look, I have to get back," she says. "I think my phone is charged now."

The pauses have been too long and too pronounced. I can't afford to hesitate any longer. I have to dive in one way or another. Just feel my way around and hope that I get a good result.

"Have you ever been to the Wagon Wheel Motel?"
I ask.

Gavin gives me an approving nod. I'm standing in the
sun and I'm starting to feel sweaty. I move into the
shaded area of the patio in front of their cabin.
Bennett turns to face me along with Gavin.

"I don't think I've been there. I just saw it. The motel
in town's pretty popular for people to go to hook up."

"Why is that?"

"They're pretty lax on checking IDs. Occasionally,
the clerk will, but sometimes they won't. I've heard of
counselors going up there and getting it on."

"Have you ever been there?"

"Not to hook up with someone, just in the area. I
rode by it of course. It's the first thing you see when
you go through the trails and you head to town, but I
never made it a stop."

"Never made it a stop?" I ask.

She shakes her head. "No."

"Can I ask you what your bike was doing outside of
the motel all night long the night that Sarah died?"

Her face drops and the smile vanishes from her lips.
She starts to breathe through her mouth and her lips
go dry.

"I don't know what you're talking about."

I don't want to argue. I do this as calmly as possible, hoping that it will elicit the truth out of her. I pull out my phone and show her bike to her. It's a video. Then we zoom in on her bike right outside.

She looks at the footage and then looks up at me. "I wasn't there."

"I find that hard to believe. You said this is your bike. You said that no one else rides it besides you. Not that I have any doubt, but does this look like your bike?"

"Yes, of course." She slumps her shoulders, looking defeated. "I don't know why it was there. I definitely didn't take it. That night I was here in bed sleeping. This footage is from what? 3:00 in the morning?"

What I don't tell her is that we couldn't find a time when the bike appeared. I scrolled through back and forth. Gavin watched every hour exactly, but I know that it was sometime after that and it had been there since at least midnight.

"If you didn't take it there and you weren't at this motel that night, who could have used it?"

Her eyes meet mine. She snorts a little bit and I realize that she's getting over a cold. Her voice is a little raspy. She heads inside the cabin. When she

starts to cough and takes a sip of water, I follow
her in.

"Like I told you before, Bennett, I'm here to find out
what happened to your friend. I'm tired of all the
lies. If you weren't involved in her murder, you need
to tell me the truth about what happened right here
and right now."

She sits down on the edge of the lower bunk. The
bed is unmade blankets pushed up against the wall.
She looks down at her water bottle and twists the top
on and then twists it off in a nervous fashion.

"I never saw Sarah that morning or that night," she
says. "She never came home. I know she had a fight
with Elizabeth. I saw the scratches on Elizabeth's
face."

"So, why did you tell me that you saw her?"

"Because I didn't want her to get in trouble. I didn't
want her to get kicked out. She had come back
initially, and if I told people that she didn't spend the
night here, Dr. Abbott would have called her parents
and she'd have to leave. I didn't know where she was,
and I was protecting her. I didn't know that anything
bad had happened."

"But you knew about the fight with Elizabeth?"

"Yes. She asked us all to say that we were all together to protect Sarah and her. She said the fight wasn't too bad. Just a stupid argument about a boy. Elizabeth was trying to get her to understand that she couldn't be so promiscuous with him, that he wouldn't respect her, and she just was so sick of waiting. She really loved him and she didn't care. Elizabeth was looking out for her."

"Do you really believe that?"

"I don't know. I did at that point. We were all close. We're friends. At least I thought we were."

"Had they ever had a fight like that before? Physical?"

"No, but they've had plenty of words. Didn't talk to each other for a week or so. I mean, this is camp. There is a lot of drama. You're friends with one girl then next week you're not friends with her anymore and it was just supposed to be something like that."

"And it wasn't?"

"I don't know."

Bennett continues to twist the cap on top of the bottle.

"We were all protecting Sarah."

"And what about when you found out that Sarah was dead? Didn't you think that it was important for you to come forward and tell me what happened?"

Bennett slumps down even further. She grabs her phone and I'm about to take it from her. I'm about to tell her to not turn it on, but she just holds it, cradling it like the way a child does with their favorite stuffed animal.

"I wasn't sure what had happened."

I deliver a blow. "Is that why you went to the motel that night? Is that why you're part of the murder?"

"I was not part of any murder. I had nothing to do with that. I hadn't seen her since the morning before. Well, maybe it was the afternoon," she says. "I can't remember exactly."

"Well, you have to because right now you're the primary suspect, Bennett. You're the only one at the scene. You all lied about the last time you saw her. Now we know that she was in the motel room that night. I also know that Dominic, the guy that she was in the motel room with, left early. He left around five, but your bike was still there. So, you stayed. After that, I know nothing except for when her body was found early the next morning by the river. How did you get her body there? What happened?"

The questions blow her back. She stares at me in disbelief.

"I had nothing to do with that. I wasn't even at the motel."

"So how was your bike there?"

"It just was," she says. "Somebody must have taken it."

"Who? Who knows the combination to the lock?"

"My roommates," she says after taking a deep breath. "They all know, and I know theirs."

"Anyone else?"

She shakes her head no. "I mean, they might have told someone, of course."

"You shouldn't have lied to me, Bennett. This conversation isn't over. If there's something else that you're not sharing, you tell me right now. Sarah deserves that much."

"No, that's it." She nods and hangs her head.

I don't believe her for a second.

33

CHARLOTTE

When I leave Bennett in the cabin, I close the door behind me. I'm steaming. She had lied about so much more than I ever anticipated, but, of course, she insisted that she wasn't at the motel at all.

"What do you think?" I ask Gavin.

"I have no idea. These teenagers are so full of lies. I can't even begin to comprehend."

"Yes, I know." I nod. "Did you ever lie like that?"

He pushes his baseball cap up from his face. The question takes him by surprise.

"I used to steal a lot. I was thirteen, fourteen, fifteen. Gas stations, department stores. Just walk in and pick up a few things. I got immunity, right, if I tell you this?"

"Wow. Yes, of course. You? You used to steal?"

"What kind of things did you take?" I ask.

"Electronics, USBs, makeup for my girl, shoes. One time my car broke down so I stole some auto parts."

"Wow. What was that like?"

"Hilarious."

"Well, then anything else?"

"No one tends to steal that kind of stuff from the shop so I think I took them by surprise."

"Yes. My older brother. He was into all the bad things that you imagine some teenagers are into. Selling drugs, gang stuff. I was living with him for a while and he was just making fun of me all the time for being a square. I started stealing stuff and it turned out I was a lot better at it than him. Never got caught. He couldn't bring himself to wear respectable clothes. Buttoned-up shirts, make yourself look like a Bible salesman. He couldn't bother with all that. He said, 'What if one of my boys saw me, you know?' But it was just a costume for me."

"And what about now and how did you stop?"

"I just realized that I didn't want it to be a costume. I just wanted to be a nice guy and whatever I stole wasn't worth it. Not even close."

"Wow," I say. "So you just gave it up?"

"Yes. Turned sixteen and just had a close call and said I'd rather retire on top."

"So, what do you think about these girls?" I ask. "And Dominic?"

We are going to get to the bottom of it. There's some truth to find amid all the lies, and once we get some real evidence about who might have done it, they're all going to sing like canaries.

The screeching tires catch my attention, but it's when they roll over the gravel and park haphazardly out from the cabin that Gavin and I really look to see who it is.

The pristine white Mercedes SL is parked on the side of the cabin, having driven all the way up the walking trail and the grass, a place where no car should be.

"Excuse me, ma'am. You're not supposed to park here," Gavin says to the woman who emerges out of the driver's seat.

Her hair, the expensive ash blonde color. Her skin is lightly tanned, and her body is toned and completely assured with its long limbs and thin shapely neck and wide shoulders. She doesn't have to introduce herself. I know immediately that she is Elizabeth's mom. What I don't know is her name. I introduce myself and Officer Gavin Skeeter going with our official titles in order to give us a sense of gravitas. Given the fact that she drove all the way here and onto the grass in front of the cabin, I get the sense that she isn't one to pay too much attention to things like that.

"It's nice to meet you. I'm Brittney Mosely," she says, giving me a slight shake of the hand, but squeezing hardly at all before pulling away and heading toward the cabin.

The man who comes out from the passenger side is dressed in a suit, his hair slicked back, about ten years older than Brittney. She's probably in her fifties, but she could easily pass for mid-thirties given how well she takes care of herself, her body and skin.

Both of them brush past me, but I catch up with the man as well and catch that his name is Walter Nguyen, the Moselys attorney.

"Can you tell me what's going on here?" I ask him. "Why did you drive the car all the way up to the cabin? Is something wrong?"

"Of course, something is wrong."

Brittney turns to face me, scrunching her arms around her torso, and that's when I notice exactly how large her hands are in comparison to the slimness of her body. This isn't unusual for models. She's easily six feet tall and probably weighs under 130 pounds. She moves in a swan-like fashion, but occasionally the anxiety and nervousness peeks in despite how straight her back and posture are.

"I'm picking up my daughter and taking her home. I can't have her staying at this place any longer given what you two are doing. You're trying to get her to admit to some horrible thing that she clearly didn't do."

She dances around, using imprecise language on purpose. She doesn't want to accuse me of accusing her daughter of murder or anything else. She had clearly been coached by the attorney.

"Your daughter is not a suspect, but her roommate was found murdered, and I'm here investigating the matter. She has kept certain things from us."

"It's her right. She doesn't have to tell you anything. There's a right to privacy in this country," Brittney snaps.

Even though I'm not holding her back, she pauses for a moment on the porch of the cabin before shaking her head and rushing in without a knock.

"Mom, what are you doing here?" I hear Elizabeth ask.

Clearly, she hadn't been notified about the upcoming plans. I don't hear the conversation or the back and forth, but after a little bit, I step onto the porch and peek in through the doorway. At first, Brittney tries to explain to her daughter why she has to leave, but when Elizabeth continues to protest, she just heads to the closet, grabs a bag, and starts stuffing her belongings into it.

"This isn't even my bag, Mom."

"I don't care. She can send us a bill."

"No, stop it."

They fight over the Louis Vuitton until finally Elizabeth grabs a similar-looking suitcase from the closet, but with different style handles, and plops it onto the lower bunk.

"I don't understand what we're doing here or why we're leaving."

"These cops, they're sniffing around. I don't want them interviewing you. You have nothing to say. Mr. Nguyen is here to help."

"He's not here to do anything but sleep with you," Elizabeth snaps.

Her mom raises her hand to smack her across the face, but she stops midway.

"You pack right now and take what you want to take. Otherwise, you're leaving without any of that stuff. You have twenty minutes."

Brittney and Walter step outside as she tries to blow off some steam. I nod to Gavin to keep them occupied and try to sneak in through the back door to talk to Elizabeth.

"Did something happen? Why is your mom here?" I ask.

"Because she's freaking out. She thinks I had some-- She thinks that--"

"Don't talk to her," Brittney says through the doorway. "Don't you dare say a word. I don't give you permission to interview my daughter," she says, turning to me. "Do you understand that she's under eighteen?"

"Yes, I understand that."

Except what Brittney doesn't quite understand is that the right extends a certain way. Her daughter has the right to have an attorney present and her mom during the conversation. The thing is that now, they are present. The question is, how do I get her to talk? How do I get her to say anything? I feel myself getting desperate. How do you get someone to admit something that you don't know that they did?

"How do you feel about your mom being here?" I ask.

"Angry. She shouldn't have come. I'm not ready to go. This whole thing with Sarah, I mean, why did it have to happen? This was supposed to be such a good summer. We were supposed to have fun."

"Do you have any idea what might have happened? Who might have done this to her?"

"No, I don't," Elizabeth says.

She packs a few of her things into the suitcase and then starts to unplug her electronics. When Brittney steps out, I take a step closer to her and say, "The thing is, Elizabeth, we have a video of you at the motel."

"What are you talking about?"

I look her straight in the eye. I bite my lower lip, appearing unsure, or perhaps disclosing that I am quite unsure over this whole thing.

"There's a video of you at the motel the night that Sarah and Dominic were there. You rode your bike there and parked it outside. That was in the middle of the night. What were you doing there? I know that you know what happened to her, and if it was an accident, you have to tell me. Your mom and that attorney, her boyfriend, are acting like they're on your side, but they're not."

This is all a blatant lie, of course. I don't have a video of her. If anything, I have a video of Bennett's bike being there. But it's not illegal for cops to lie to get confessions out of people, and a lie like this will go a long way in telling me the extent of what this girl knows.

"I saw you on camera," I say, talking quietly but sternly. "I know that you know what happened to Sarah."

I don't go so far as to say that we have footage of what had happened because, frankly, I don't know if it happened at the motel or at the shore, but the killer would.

Elizabeth's eyes start to dart from side to side. The façade of the cool, popular girl who has it all together starts to fade. She sits down on the edge of the bunk bed and stares somewhere out in the distance for a moment. She turns into the teenager that she is. The twenty-something affect disappears. It's almost like the inner child that she has been hiding all along, pretending it wasn't there, emerges.

"You can tell me what happened, Elizabeth. I'm here to help you. I just need an explanation."

"She wasn't supposed to be there," she says, taking big inhales, trying to push the snot that's coming out of her nose along with the tears back in. "I had told her to stay away from *him*."

"Dominic?" I ask.

"After we had that fight, I kept waiting for her to come home and then she didn't. I just knew that she had to be with him. She'd called him and they were together."

"You went?"

This was over a boy, I think to myself. How stupid. People die over stupidity like this every day, however.

"You followed them?"

"Yes. I took Bennett's bike and I rode it down there. I didn't want mine to be caught on camera, so I took hers."

I swallow hard; she did it. She's the one. She hid it so well. If it weren't for my lie, she wouldn't be saying any of this.

She stops talking for a moment, collecting her thoughts. I don't dare to turn back and break the trance that we have here. I pray silently that her mom and her lawyer don't show back up before I hear the end of the story.

"You followed? You went back to the motel room where you thought they went?"

She nods.

"What happened then?"

"I didn't know which room they were in, but I saw their bikes. I parked Bennett's a little bit out of the way so they wouldn't see it. They stayed there until like five. It was terrible. I was planning on leaving. Every hour, I told myself that it wasn't worth it, that I should just go, but I couldn't bring myself to do it."

"What happened when they came out?"

"Dominic came out first, and he grabbed his bike and he rode off."

"They didn't come out together?" I ask.

She shakes her head. "No."

I remember that is exactly what I had seen on camera.

"I was going to talk to both of them, but then when it was just her, I don't know, it was probably better that way."

"What were you planning on talking to her about?"

"Just the same thing, that she shouldn't have slept with him, that he wasn't hers."

"Did you have a crush on him?"

"Yes, I guess. We had flirted back and forth, but he and Misty had this complicated thing. He said that he wanted to hook up this summer, but then with Sarah being so in love with him, it felt weird. I just didn't want her to like him."

"What about your girlfriend, Erica?"

"I don't have a girlfriend. She was just a girl."

The way she responds and snaps at me at the insinuation makes me rethink my approach. I don't want her to get angry. Pushing her on whether or not she was dating a girl is not a priority here.

"What I need to know is what happened to Sarah. What happened when Sarah came out?" I ask.

"I followed her down the trail and then she turned and went a little way toward the shore. She took another trail to where the dock was. I don't know. I guess she was going to watch the sunrise or something. That's when I followed her out. At first, it was cordial. I almost apologized for earlier, but then she just wouldn't tell me what happened with her and Dominic. She said it was none of my business. I guess it wasn't, but I was so angry."

"What happened then, Elizabeth?"

"She told me to go away. She threw a rock at me, and it hit my shoulder and it scared me, so I lunged at her. We started fighting just like before, but then... it was an accident, you have to believe me. My mom doesn't want me to tell you, but it was all an accident."

"Did you tell your mom this?"

"Yes, of course, when it happened. She told me that I had to stay here and act like nothing was wrong. She told me the whole story to come up with, but this isn't right. I didn't do it on purpose. It was an accident. You have to believe me."

"What happened *exactly*?" I ask.

"Sarah hit her head on a rock. I was shaking her, and I guess I had my hands around her neck and maybe I squeezed too tight. I don't know, it's all a blur, but I didn't mean for her to die. I didn't mean for anything to happen."

"What happened then, Elizabeth?" I continue to press, cold blood rushing through my body, my hands turning to ice.

She had killed her friend and she had told her mother what happened, and her mother told her to stay, make up a lie, get everyone on her side, and make up a cover story.

"Mom told me that I had to move her body somewhere else to hide the evidence or something. That she wouldn't be able to help me, but I had to do it. She walked me through it, and I did. I moved her as far as I could. I was supposed to put her in the lake, but the sun was starting to come up. Joggers started to show up, I was afraid they were going to catch me, so I submerged her as well as I could. Then I had to go. It was morning and I couldn't deal with it anymore."

Tears stream down her face. Suddenly, Gavin yells my name and Brittney shows up in the doorway. I guess he'd held on and kept her attention for as long as he could.

"What are you doing?" Brittney snaps at her daughter.

"I told her everything, Mom."

"Shut up!" Brittney yells at her daughter. "Don't say another word. None of this counts," Brittney snaps at me, pointing her finger in my face.

"She's underage, but you're not," I say. "Officer Skeeter, place this woman under arrest, please. Confiscate her phone. I have a feeling that when we run the phone records, we'll find out that your daughter called you around five thirty a.m., the morning of Sarah's murder, and told you exactly what happened, and you told her how to cover up her tracks and what lies to tell to get away with this."

"You have no proof of any of this. Let go of me."

"Mrs. Mosely, I'd advise you to please stop resisting arrest. Otherwise, we will have to add more charges," Gavin says in a calm and direct manner.

Walter Nguyen leans over and whispers something into his girlfriend's ear. She clenches her jaw and stands up straight, letting Gavin put the cuffs around her.

"I have a feeling that when the DNA evidence comes back from Sarah, we'll find out that your daughter was the one who killed her."

"She had nothing to do with this!" Brittney yells.

"This is a mistake. It was an accident," Elizabeth moans, tears running from her eyes down her cheeks as she cries, as her sobs get louder and louder.

"Shut up, you stupid girl. Shut up."

34

SARAH

S arah had woken up early that morning in a state of fog. It was kind of like what happened when you woke up from a nap that you shouldn't have taken in the first place, a little bit confused as to where you were, what you were doing, and how you even got there. But when she reached over and saw the guy lying next to her and that it was Dominic, memories immediately flooded back. She snuggled up to him. He wrapped his arms around her. Even though they both stood the chance of getting kicked out of camp for good and disgracefully sent home with whatever little measly pay they received, on some level she knew that being here right now would make it worth it.

It was close to four o'clock then, and after a good fifteen minutes of her staring at him, Dominic opened his eyes, feeling that uncertain pressure of her glare.

"You know in some cultures that's considered rather rude."

"Not mine." She laughed, giving him a kiss.

He kissed her back. She wanted to ask him more than anything what this meant for them, where they stood as far as the relationship goes, but she didn't want to be that girl either. She wanted to enjoy being with him at this moment in time because after all, she didn't sleep with him for him to make her any promises. She didn't sleep with him for clout.

"I just want you to know that this was really nice," Dominic said. "I had a really good time and I don't say that lightly."

"Me, too." She smiled.

"I'm still worried about you going back to your roommate though, the bruises."

"Let's not talk about her now," Sarah cut him off. She wanted to make this space apart from Elizabeth, something that didn't have her fingerprints on it or her DNA.

"I think it'd be best if we left at different times," she said, getting up from the bed to use the bathroom. Dominic clearly didn't understand. When she came back out again and washed her hands, splashing some water on her face, she turned to face him, still wrapped in the top sheet that she stole from the bed.

"I just don't think that anyone should see us coming back to camp together. So maybe you take off now, I'll take a shower, wait a little bit, and just meet you at breakfast."

"You're going to stay? You're going to stay and take a nap?"

"No." Sarah shook her head. "I might ride down to the shore, watch the sunrise, that kind of thing. Something corny."

"Let me come with you."

"No. I mean, of course, I want you to, but I'll see you later. I'll see you tomorrow and maybe we can go on a date."

"I'd like that." Dominic nodded.

He got ready to go, sliding into his jeans, popping a T-shirt over his head. She got dressed as well, and right before he left, he kneeled down to kiss her and she asked him for a favor.

"It's nothing big, but given how Elizabeth reacted, can we just keep this a secret for a little bit, you and me dating or whatever this is? I just don't want anyone to know, you know?"

"I get it."

"Can you please not tell your roommates, friends, random campers?"

"So, you don't want me to brag about taking you to bed tonight in a hotel room?"

"No, I don't." Sarah smiled. "Besides, you know that if anyone were to find out about the motel, they would totally kick us out."

"Yes, against regulation and all."

Dominic smiled and gave her a wink. He flashed his pearly whites, and she knew that things had changed between them for the better. Things would never be the same, and that would be a good thing.

"I really like you, Sarah," Dominic said, grabbing her hand, intertwining his fingers with hers. "There's something about this that makes sense and I'm not going to tell anyone about any of it. I just want you to know."

"Good." She smiled and swallowed hard. Something felt odd. The heaviness was pressing down on her. She didn't know what it was. It felt strange at the same time. What she had not known was that this would be the last time that she would see Dominic again and this would be the last time that he would see her alive.

Sarah had waited a good bit of time prior to leaving the motel. She flipped through the channels. She tried to sleep some more but none of it worked. She checked to make sure that she had everything with her. She didn't bother sleeping because she knew she wouldn't stay long enough. Less than fifteen minutes later, she made her way out to her bike and onto the trail.

That was the first time that she felt like someone was following her. She knew better than to wear her AirPods in the forest area. She didn't want to think but she liked having something else to think about and she popped them in her ears, nevertheless.

Still, somewhere in the background, she felt the presence. She pulled them out, slowed down, and listened carefully as her wheels went over the loose branches on the trail that she knew that Dominic had just followed. Then the twig broke in half. She turned and, from behind the bend, she heard something.

"Hello?" she yelled out. "I know you're there. Stop following me."

She tried to keep her voice from shaking but there wasn't much she could do.

"Hey, it's just me," a familiar voice said, and she immediately let out a sigh of relief.

"What are you doing here, Elizabeth?"

"I was just-"

"Spying on me?" she finished the line for her.

Sarah started to peddle not wanting to engage. She stood up on her pedals and started to try to go as fast as possible.

"Listen, wait!" Elizabeth yelled after her, struggling to keep up.

Her bike wasn't as good, didn't have as many gears, and the trail got a little tricky. Sarah tried to lose her. She took a different trail that led closer to the lake and then immediately realized her mistake because she knew that that was where the trail would end in the water.

"Sarah, please wait!" Elizabeth yelled after her.

Finally, she stopped without getting off her bike. She folded her arms across her chest.

"Why are you following me? Why are you stalking me?" she asked.

"I'm not. I just need to talk to you. I'm really sorry about how we left things."

"Yes, me, too. So, let's just not talk about it anymore."

Sarah was fuming on the inside but tried to keep her anger away. She had no right to look for her.

Sarah stood up on the pedals and started to go faster and faster. Elizabeth was having a hard time keeping up. Bennett's bike was not in as good a shape and she didn't have gears the way that Sarah did, but she had made a mistake. She veered closer to the lake, and that was where Elizabeth had caught up with her.

"I just want to talk to you!" she yelled across the way.

"Leave me alone!" Sarah yelled back.

Elizabeth wouldn't leave it alone. She needed to be heard. She was used to getting what she wanted. Sarah made a slightly wrong turn. Something caught underneath her front tire and when she tried to overcorrect she landed on her side, her bike underneath, pinning her on top. She winced in pain and Elizabeth rushed over. She had scraped up a little bit of her leg, but as soon as she saw her roommate standing above her, she started to try to get out of the way.

"I don't want to have a fight with you. What do you want me to say?"

"That's not what I'm trying to do here," Elizabeth said, extending her hand to help her up.

Sarah just pushed it away. She rose up to her feet, grabbed onto her bike only to discover that the tire had been punctured and the rim was bent.

"Look what you made me do," she snapped. "You want to talk to me so badly? Go ahead. What? What is so important?"

"I just want to talk to you about Dominic."

"No, I'm not talking about him. We can agree to disagree, but it's none of your business whatever has happened."

"What did happen?" Elizabeth asked.

"It's none of your *freaking* business!" she yelled, her words echoing around the lake.

She started to walk away, but Elizabeth couldn't leave it at that. She couldn't make her talk. She couldn't let her engage, and she wanted to piss her off, but how? She had picked up a small pebble from the ground and threw it at her friend. It hit her shoulder.

"What are you doing?" she snapped.

Sarah bent down and grabbed a large rock the size of her palm.

"You're throwing rocks at me? Are you serious?"

Before she finished talking, she threw it at Elizabeth, missing her head by barely an inch. The rock nearly missing her pushed her over the edge. She lunged herself at Sarah, pushing her onto the ground.

Sarah was caught by surprise and tried to fight back, but Elizabeth was taller, longer, and stronger. When she shook her by the shoulders, Sarah's head bobbed up and down on the rocky shoreline. The first time she hit her head, she felt a little dizzy. The second time, she couldn't fight back as much, but Elizabeth kept yelling.

She kept saying, "Why wouldn't you listen to me? He's using you over and over again," while wrapping her hands around her friend's throat.

Elizabeth was so upset, disoriented, and out of control that she hadn't realized that Sarah hadn't been fighting back for the last thirty seconds. Her body had gone limp with no air coming in. Her arms lay by her sides listlessly.

When Elizabeth realized what she had done, she lost herself in stunned-like silence. She stared at the suddenly diminutive body of her friend who lay lifelessly before her.

A couple of beats passed, hysteria mixed with sadness, anger, and disappointment rushed in. She grabbed onto her friend. She held her tight. She cradled her head. She pleaded louder and louder for her to come back.

"Please, please, please," she cried as she shook her shoulders and hit her head harder on the rocks underneath.

Somewhere over the horizon over the mountains, she saw a brief twinkle of light. The sun would come out soon.

With that, someone would find out what she had done. She grabbed her phone and called the one person who might help her keep this secret hidden.

35

CHARLOTTE

The DNA scraped from underneath Sarah Dunn's fingernails come back with proof that it was Elizabeth Mosely with whom she had had that fight by the lake. The records pulled from her phone and her mother's phone also confirmed the conversation matching the time and date of the one she would've called her after committing the murder. Then there's the confession which may or may not get thrown out of court depending on how skillful her lawyer is, but that I will not know for quite some time.

In the meantime, Elizabeth is booked and awaiting trial, released on two million dollar bond to her father's custody with her passport confiscated. Her mother is awaiting trial on her own charges of accessory, interfering with prosecution, et cetera.

The mystery is solved, so to speak. The questions linger, and the sadness in Sarah's parents' eyes is ever-present.

They've come to talk to me a few times and called me on my phone a few more. Her mother mostly being the one to stay in touch. I reassure her, explain the procedure, and give her the number of the assistant district attorney, hoping that she gets the hint to call her from now on. As far as Dominic is concerned, he came really close to being the primary suspect and the one to take the fall for this. He had lied to me multiple times. He did everything and anything but cooperate, and he hid things from me that made me think that it was probably him.

When we talk after Elizabeth's arrest and I prep him a little bit for the trial and what to expect, he looks solemn and detached, not like the guy that I remember meeting earlier. He's back at school starting his senior year planning to apply to colleges all over California and the East Coast with no specific plans on one particular one.

"I used to think that I would stay around here forever," he says to me. We meet up at a coffee shop back in Palm Valley when he visits the area with his friends for a weekend. "Now I wonder if going as far away from California as possible would be the right thing to do. I even applied to school in Hawaii and

Alaska. I guess I'll just have to visit them, see what they're all about. See how I'm feeling when it's time to go."

"Yes, that's probably right. It's rough what you've been through."

"I just have so many regrets, you know. I liked Sarah for a long time and I should have tried to be with her earlier, gotten to known her better. I shouldn't have tried so hard to be this popular, cool kid with the perfect girlfriend like Misty, and I shouldn't have ignored my feelings for Sarah, no matter how she looked or what kind of social status she had or didn't have. It's stupid to admit now and I feel like a fool. I missed out on so much time with someone that I could have really had a connection with."

"Things like that happen a lot." I nod.

"You mean I should expect future dates to get murdered as well?"

"No, I'm not saying that exactly, but you know what I mean. You have to seize life. You have to go after what you want when you want it. Life's precious. You just never know what's waiting for you around the bend."

"Can I ask you something?" I add after a long pause.

He nods, slouching in his seat, somewhat cradling the cup of coffee in between his hands the way that a child would. "Why did you keep lying to me about being the last one to see her, being in the motel with her, all that stuff? Why did I have to pull that out of you?"

"Because she didn't want anyone to know. She made me promise, and I wanted to keep that promise."

"On some level I'm glad that you kept your word, but in the future, I have to tell you that is a dangerous thing to do."

"Isn't it dangerous to confess things to cops anyway, talk to them without a lawyer?"

"Yes, you're right about that."

"Well, I'm planning on staying as far away from law enforcement as possible from now on."

"Good. That's probably the best thing."

We leave things on good terms. When I return home later that evening, I tell Dylan about this.

We have dinner and over a few containers of takeout, Thai of course, he asks, "Are you ever planning on asking me to move in with you?"

I look up mid-bite, chewing and reaching for more panang curry.

"What are you talking about?"

"Well, I've been sleeping over here for close to a month now. I figured one of these days you'd ask me to move in so I can stop paying rent over there, but maybe not. I don't want to intrude."

"Actually, I honestly haven't thought about it. I mean, I like having you here, a lot, but yes, that only makes sense."

"How romantic." Dylan smiles.

I tilt my head to one side, finish my bite, and put the fork down.

"Well, you know me. If I'm anything, I'm a hopeless romantic. You know, one of these days, I'm going to turn you into one."

He leans over the table and gives me a big kiss.

"It's all going to work out, Charlotte. You know that, right?"

I take a deep breath. He presses down on my shoulders, and I realize just how tense and scrunched up they are.

"You can't carry the weight of the world," he says. "You can't worry about everything. You've got to learn how to compartmentalize things, put your emotions about this case in a bucket, shove it somewhere deep and dark, and forget about it until the trial comes up."

"You know, that's the opposite of what therapists say," I point out.

"I'm just trying to offer some advice that I can't really follow myself."

I tilt my head, and the mood changes. He's not so much giving me advice but commiserating. I know that he has been through this whole bunch of shit as well.

"Yes, I can't dwell on every case," I say, "and in this situation she was already dead when I found her. It's a little bit different from the missing persons and unsolved mysteries that plague me at night."

He swallows hard. I narrow my eyes. I realize that we're talking about two different things.

"Are you thinking about your brother again?" I ask.

He gives me a nod.

"His birthday's coming up. He's still gone, never to be heard from again."

"Putting things in compartments and shoving them into a dark place in your closet, that's what? Advice for *you* rather than me?"

"Sounds about right." Dylan nods.

Then it's my turn to reach over the table and give him a kiss. My phone vibrates on the table. I'm about to send it to voice mail when I see the number.

"Kelsey. I haven't talked to her for a little bit. Do you mind if I take this call?"

"Of course not. I'm going to go get some more food."

He walks to the kitchen and piles more rice and Pad Thai onto his plate.

"It's good to hear from you," I say.

Kelsey and I catch up for a few minutes, and then she suddenly says, "Hey, I was thinking, now that your case is over, loose ends all pretty much tied up, would you mind going to Seattle with me for the weekend? I need to talk to my parents. I need to play all this out and put it to bed."

"Yes, of course," I say. "Let's do that."

THANK you for reading Girl in the Lake. I hope you have enjoyed it. Want to know what happens next? Make sure to download the FREE Lake of Lies novella (to get onto my newsletter list) and be notified when the next book in the Charlotte Pierce series will be released (it's coming soon!)

Can't get enough? Read LAKE OF LIES (A Detective Charlotte Pierce novella) for FREE!

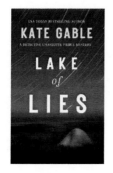

SPECIAL REQUEST: Please make sure to take a moment to leave a review on the retailer of your choice. Reviews really help me find more readers and to keep writing.

If you find any issues or mistakes or typos, please feel free to reach out to me directly at Kate@kategable.com This way I can address them as soon as possible.

Thank you for reading and supporting my work!

Kate

BE THE FIRST TO KNOW ABOUT MY UPCOMING SALES, NEW RELEASES AND EXCLUSIVE GIVEAWAYS!

W ant a Free book? Sign up for my Newsletter!

Sign up for my newsletter:

https://www.subscribepage.com/kategableviplist

Join my Facebook Group:
https://www.facebook.com/groups/833851020557518

Bonus Points: Follow me on BookBub and
Goodreads!

https://www.goodreads.com/author/show/21534224.
Kate_Gable

ABOUT KATE GABLE

Kate Gable loves a good mystery that is full of suspense. She grew up devouring psychological thrillers and crime novels as well as movies, tv shows and true crime.

Her favorite stories are the ones that are centered on families with lots of secrets and lies as well as many twists and turns. Her novels have elements of psychological suspense, thriller, mystery and romance.

Kate Gable lives near Palm Springs, CA with her husband, son, a dog and a cat. She has spent more than twenty years in Southern California and finds inspiration from its cities, canyons, deserts, and small mountain towns.

She graduated from University of Southern California with a Bachelor's degree in Mathematics. After pursuing graduate studies in mathematics, she switched gears and got her MA in Creative Writing and English from Western New Mexico University and her PhD in Education from Old Dominion University.

Writing has always been her passion and obsession. Kate is also a USA Today Bestselling author of romantic suspense under another pen name.

Write her here:

Kate@kategable.com

Check out her books here:

www.kategable.com

Sign up for my newsletter:
https://www.subscribepage.com/kategableviplist

Join my Facebook Group:
https://www.facebook.com/groups/833851020557518

Bonus Points: Follow me on BookBub and Goodreads!

https://www.bookbub.com/authors/kate-gable

https://www.goodreads.com/author/show/21534224.Kate_Gable

amazon.com/Kate-Gable/e/B095XFCLL7

facebook.com/kategablebooks

bookbub.com/authors/kate-gable

instagram.com/kategablebooks

ALSO BY KATE GABLE

All books are available at ALL major retailers! If you can't find it, please email me at
kate@kategable.com
www.kategable.com

Detective Kaitlyn Carr

Girl Missing (Book 1)
Girl Lost (Book 2)
Girl Found (Book 3)
Girl Taken (Book 4)
Girl Forgotten (Book 5)

Girl Hidden (FREE Novella)
Lake of Lies (FREE Novella)

Detective Charlotte Pierce

Last Breath
Nameless Girl
Missing Lives
Girl in the Lake

Lake of Lies (FREE Novella)

Made in United States
North Haven, CT
16 February 2024

48838290R00187